THE GAME CAPTURES
THE HUNTER...

"I had the idea that we can pick a time when all
the outlaws are in the hideout and blow up the arch
at the mouth of the box canyon. If we seal the
opening, there's no place on the walls for them to
climb out."

"You're right," Ki assured Jessie.

"I brought back what we need to do it," Jessie said.

"Gunpowder?" Ki asked.

"No. A new explosive. It's called dynamite..."

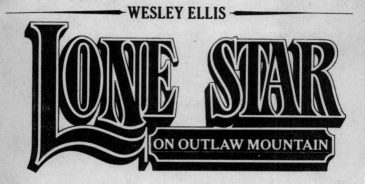

WESLEY ELLIS

LONE STAR

ON OUTLAW MOUNTAIN

A JOVE BOOK

LONE STAR ON OUTLAW MOUNTAIN

A Jove Book / published by arrangement with
the author

PRINTING HISTORY
Jove edition / May 1983

ISBN: 0-515-06236-7

★

Chapter 1

Bathed in the bright hot Southwest Texas sunshine of a late summer afternoon, Jessie and Ki reached the top of the ridge and pulled up their horses. A mile or so ahead of them, strands of barbwire stood out in metallic streaks as harsh as the landscape itself. The wire made three sharp horizontal lines against the fading green patch that was the only fenced enclosure on the sprawling Circle Star ranch.

Far beyond the first barbwire strands they could see the ranch's boundary fence, almost hidden from view by the shimmering heat haze. The sun glowed on the backs and picked out the polished tips of the horns of the cattle that moved aimlessly between the two fences, but most of the animals in the breeding-bull pasture were clustered around the small springfed stock pond that glistened in its center.

"They look good from here, Ki," Jessie told her companion as she pushed her wide-brimmed hat back from her forehead. "But I won't say I'm satisfied until I get a closer look."

"I didn't think you just wanted an excuse to take a ride," Ki said. "I know how important it is to breed heavier steers. If we don't keep up with what the King

1

Ranch is doing down on the Gulf, the Circle Star cattle won't keep bringing top prices."

"Of course I'm interested in the bulls," Jessie replied. "But we've been gone from the ranch so much lately that I've almost forgotten how wonderful it is here. And I don't propose to let anything keep us from staying through the roundup, because that's the best time of year to be here."

They sat for a few moments to let the horses breathe after the long upslope ride, then moved on toward the fence.

Jessie Starbuck felt at peace with the world as her favorite horse, the palomino named Sun, covered the level ground in effortless strides. Because there had been no direct attack on the Circle Star since her father was murdered there, Jessie was not wearing her gunbelt. She missed the solid weight of the Colt against her hip, for she'd carried the gun almost continuously since Alex's death. Today, when she and Ki had started out, she'd decided that the rifle in her saddle scabbard was enough.

Alex Starbuck's assassination had been the cue for a series of efforts by the vicious agents of an unscrupulous European-based cartel to try to wrest away the vast Starbuck holdings.

Jessie's delicately molded nostrils expanded as she inhaled the warm air, and her full red lips curled into a contented smile in spite of the glare of the sun that kept her lids slitted to shield her lustrous green eyes.

She was wearing the clothing in which she felt most comfortable, a lightweight cotton blouse that did nothing to hide the provocative fullness of her breasts, tight-fitting jeans tucked into high-heeled range boots, and a wide-brimmed Stetson that shaded the cream-smooth skin of her lightly tanned face. As was her habit when on the ranch, she'd bound her shoulder-length, coppery blonde hair with a simple jade-and-gold clasp and let it fall free down her back. It rippled in the breeze under the brim of her hat as she and Ki rode at a leisurely pace toward the fenced pasture.

Ki shared Jessie's feeling of ease, though in his case it did not come from the freedom of his clothing or from the lack of a holstered revolver at his hip. Ki wore his usual attire: a well-worn black leather vest over a loose cotton shirt and denim jeans. His shoes were a pair of black cotton slippers with rope soles.

Ki, in fact, seldom wore a gunbelt. As a general rule, he disdained the use of firearms, feeling that most men who used them became overly dependent upon them; it was one of the tenets of his lifelong training as a warrior that a man should never become too fond of any one weapon, since it would never be appropriate to all occasions. As a result, although on this day he did not carry his slim *ko-dachi* blade tucked into the waistband of his trousers, he did have tucked into the pockets of his vest *shuriken* blades of two sizes, deadly, star-shaped throwing blades of steel, with points and edges as finely honed as a surgeon's scalpel. The innocent-looking rope that he wore as a belt was tipped at either end with a leather-covered iron ball; it was a *surushin,* not usually a deadly weapon but one that could be thrown to entangle and immobilize an opponent until Ki closed in.

Remaining inconspicuous was a problem for Ki, especially in the more sparsely populated areas of the West. He was half Japanese and half American, and the Oriental side of his heritage was visible in the sallow tone of his skin and in the upturned corners of his eyes, as well as in the straight, almost blue-black hair that hung to his shoulders. Though his shirt fit him loosely, concealing the powerful muscles beneath it, he radiated a sense of strength. As striking as Ki and Jessie were as individuals, when they traveled together they were not easily ignored or forgotten. And they traveled together often; it might

3

even be said that they were inseparable, Ki in his role of Jessie Starbuck's friend, confidant, servant, protector, and teacher, though in the case of the last, it was certainly true that Ki learned as much from Jessie as she from him.

Now he said, "I haven't heard Ed say anything about when the roundup's going to start this year. Has he mentioned it to you?"

"No. I've been intending to ask him, but since we got back I've just been enjoying resting too much to look ahead. He'll tell us when he decides, and I'm not going to worry about it until he sets the time."

In companionable silence the pair rode on to the barbwire fence. They reined in and looked at the breeding bulls.

At close range, the animals scattered around the stock pond presented an astonishingly varied appearance. Some were longhorns, their hides ranging from a creamy tan to a chocolate brown so dark that in some lights the bulls looked black. Among them were a small number of the mouse-gray shade called grulla, and a few were ticked with patternless dark dots on a cream or light tan background hue. All the longhorns were the same in their body formation: rangy of leg, with deep but narrow chests; thin in the flanks, with outspread horns that were measured in feet from tip to tip. All were direct descendants of the Asturian cattle brought over by the Spanish conquistadores three centuries earlier, when they began to colonize what was then called New Spain.

Longhorns made up roughly half of the breeding-bull herd. The other half were uniform in color: a deep brownish red with a white marking that began just behind their shoulders and extended in a curving, symmetrical sweep around their forequarters to their bellies. These bulls were stocky, with legs so short that their wide, deep chests

4

nearly touched the ground, heavy in their flanks and hind legs; they were Herefords of British breeding.

Scattered across the pasture were still other bulls that showed the characteristics of both longhorn and Hereford. Their horns were short, but still had a wider span than did those of the purebred bulls, and the configuration of their bodies shared the traits of both strains. These were the bulls to which Jessie and Ki paid the closest attention.

Like owners of many of the big Texas spreads, Alex Starbuck had begun before his death to set the Circle Star to work on a program of crossbreeding, trying to produce cattle meatier than the longhorn but having the breed's survival instincts and resistance to disease. Jessie had kept the work of crossbreeding going, for of all the properties she'd inherited from Alex, the Circle Star was to her what it had been to him, the place closest to their hearts.

"Yes, we're making progress," Jessie said with a smile of satisfaction as she surveyed the cattle. "The legs of some of the crossbreeds are still too short for range cattle, but they've got horns enough to defend themselves from wolves, and good meaty hindquarters. Ed's done a good job since he took over as foreman from Dave Clemson."

Ki nodded, but said nothing. Looking at the crossbred bulls reminded him of his own mixed ancestry, and what it had cost him. His *samurai* grandfather had driven his daughter, Ki's mother, from the family home. Ki had grown up as an outcast, bitter at the prejudice that had made him a stranger in his own land and had led to his emigration to America, where he'd drifted until finding a steady anchor with Alex Starbuck, who had been a family friend during Starbuck's early ventures in Oriental trade.

Jessie did not notice Ki's silence. Her attention had

been caught by one of the crossbred bulls, more longhorn than Hereford in body and color. The bull had appeared with startling suddenness, running over a little hump beyond the stock pond. He covered the ground with a strange stumbling gait. His eyes were glazed and expanded to show their yellowish rims, and his tongue hung out, long thick strings of foamy slobber dripping from it. As the bull ran, it blatted almost constantly, a broken series of drawn-out, nasal grunting noises that could have expressed almost anything from discomfort to anger.

"Why, that bull is sick, Ki!" Jessie exclaimed. "He's got to be isolated from the others right away, or he might infect the whole herd. We've put too much time and money into this crossbreeding project to have that happen!"

Before Ki could answer, Jessie had swung out of her saddle and was running across the short distance that separated them from the fence. She angled toward the nearest post as she ran, and, placing her hands on the post, vaulted the fence with ease and skill.

"Jessie!" Ki called as he saw what she intended to do. "Don't go into the pasture on foot! Those longhorns are—"

He broke off, for by this time Jessie was on the other side of the fence and still heading for the blatting steer. The other bulls had begun to stir when the crazed animal first appeared. Those that had been lying down were on their feet, swinging their heads nervously from side to side. The bulls that had been on their feet were turning in the direction of the zigzag path described by the running animal.

Ki knew he was wasting breath by calling again. He also remembered what Jessie had forgotten in her excitement: that not even range steers, although half-tamed by castration when calves, would charge a mounted rider. A person on foot, however, was to them a strange sort

6

of animal representing an unknown danger. Anyone in a range herd on foot was in imminent danger of being gored and trampled to death.

In spite of this, Ki did not hesitate. He dropped from his horse, raced to the fence, vaulted it, and ran after Jessie.

Excited by the wild blatting and strange antics of the bull that had just appeared, the other animals were now beginning to mill, forming a wide circle around the strange bull. They did not appear to have noticed Jessie, who had now almost reached the oddly behaving animal, and were giving the blatting bull a wide berth, but their shifting formed a barrier between Jessie and Ki.

He stopped just short of running into the animals, and even though he knew that the sound of his voice might increase the panic that was beginning to seize the bulls, he called again.

"Jessie! Stop right where you are! Lie down flat and keep still! I'll get to you as fast as I can!"

Jessie either did not hear him or was by now aware of the danger she'd gotten into. She did not stop moving, but did move more slowly, keeping her eyes fixed on the slavering animal in front of her. The bull had stopped its advance, but Ki could not tell from its stance whether it had halted because Jessie was in its path and still walking slowly toward it, or whether its feet had grown too unsteady to allow it to move. The bull was standing with its hooves spread wide apart, its body swaying, its head with the wickedly pointed horns swinging from side to side.

Ki began picking his way through the ring of moving cattle that blocked his way to Jessie's side. There was no way for him to move unobtrusively, but the animals had not yet responded to the herd instinct that causes cattle to press together in a solid mass and stampede in times of danger.

7

Ki dodged between them, trying to avoid passing too closely in front of their heads. Once or twice one of the bulls noticed him and shied away with a throaty snort, but most of them seemed unaware of his presence. In the quick glimpses that Ki could get of Jessie while he tried to pick his way among the milling cattle, he could see that she was still a dozen yards from the bull that was threatening her.

As Ki ran, he slid a *shuriken* from his vest pocket, even though he knew he could not throw the weapon with enough force to penetrate the bull's thick hide at a vital spot. He reached the edge of the constantly moving bunch of cattle between himself and Jessie just as the crazed bull lowered its head and charged her.

Jessie dropped to the ground and rolled to one side. Ki now had a clear field. He threw the *shuriken*. The flat, star-shaped blade went true to its target, the eye of the charging bull. One of the points pierced the pupil. Blinded in one eye, the animal was drawn in the direction it could see. It turned aside from the straight line of its charge. The knife-edged hooves of its forefeet struck the ground inches from Jessie's prone body, and by the time its rush had carried its body forward, Jessie had rolled out of the way of its thudding hind feet.

Ki was at Jessie's side an instant after the bull had passed. He leaned over and grasped her wrist, and dragged her to her feet. The crazed bull was circling aimlessly through the other animals of the herd, turning in a circle in the direction it could see. Its blatting had become a wild, continuous bellowing of pain, and now the other bulls began to follow it, their horns clashing as they crowded together into a compact mass, adding their own throaty lowing to the confusion of sound. The panic that was impelling them was almost visible, hanging like a cloud that could be seen as well as sensed in the still air of the hot summer afternoon.

"What are we—" Jessie began.

Ki gave her no time to finish her question. "The stock pond," he said urgently, pulling her at a run in the direction of the little pool of water.

There were only a few scattered animals between them and the pond, but they presented a source of danger. Any of them was likely to charge at a moving object. After Ki and Jessie had covered a few yards, she began running without Ki's help, and they had little difficulty dodging the isolated bulls that were wandering aimlessly between them and the pond. They waded out into the water. The bottom of the pond shelved gently. It was at most four feet deep in the center, where the spring welled up. When Ki and Jessie were standing waist-deep, they stopped. Now fifteen feet of water stretched on all sides of them.

"We'll be safe enough here," Ki told Jessie as they stood in the cool water. "If any of those lone bulls charge us now, they'll be slowed down and stop when they get in the water."

"I wasn't sure for a minute that I was going to be able to dodge that bull's horns," Jessie said. Her voice was as calm as though death had not brushed close to her only seconds earlier. "If you hadn't been so close, I'd have been in real trouble."

Jessie did not need to thank Ki, and Ki did not expect her to. They'd shared enough close scrapes to make thanks a useless formality between them. Had Ki been in Jessie's place, she would have rushed to help him with equal swiftness.

"You'd have thought of something," Ki replied.

"It was a foolish move," Jessie said, shaking her head. "I didn't even stop to think that I didn't have my Colt. All I had in my mind was the damage that wild bull could do to the breeding herd."

They looked around. The crazed bull was silent now, except for an occasional, ear-piercing blat of pain. It had stopped circling and stood motionless. The *shuriken* was lodged in its eye socket, and around the edges, where the blade had cut into its flesh, blood was seeping, running down the animal's dewlaps in a crimson trickle. The herd instinct was working on the other bulls now. They were stopping, packing into a solid mass behind the one they'd been drawn to follow.

Ki studied the terrain between the pond and the fence. On the other side of the fence the horses stood; the commotion made by the bulls had not disturbed them. Between the pond and the fence lay a strip of ground a little more than a hundred yards wide, sloping gently upward. Because it was near the pond, it had been grazed until the ground was barren of any growth. A half-dozen bulls that had not joined the others when they formed the herd were in the bare strip. Two of the bulls were longhorns, the other four were Herefords.

Now the herd was showing signs of breaking up. Already a few of the animals were drifting off. Some of them in the rear had started in the direction of the boundary fence and were beginning to graze again. Several were ambling in the direction of the pond. Both Ki and Jessie knew that the panic which had caught them up so suddenly a few minutes earlier could be revived with equal swiftness.

"I'm going to run for the fence," Ki said. "I'll get your rifle and shoot the bull. As soon as it's dead, the others will quiet down."

With her eyes, Jessie measured the distance between the pond and the fence. She did not try to dissuade Ki; she knew her words would be wasted. Instead she asked, "Are you sure you can make it? If one of those longhorns charges—"

"I'll be going fast enough to outrun it," Ki assured her.

He began wading to the edge of the pond, moving

slowly so that he would not attract the attention of one of the animals in the strip between him and the fence. A yard from dry land, Ki stopped. The moment of greatest danger would be in the first few steps he took, after he left the pond and before he'd gained enough speed to outdistance one of the longhorns if it took a notion to charge. He did not worry about the Herefords; they were placid and tame compared to the others. He stepped from the water and stood for a moment on the dry ground. Then he began to run.

Only one of the longhorns noticed Ki, and it did not move. He made the sprint to the fence in seconds, and vaulted over the top barbwire strand. He took Jessie's rifle from her saddle scabbard and went back to the fence. The crazed bull was beginning to move again, its legs working disjointedly, its massive head swaying. Ki wasted no time. One quick shot at the base of the animal's skull, behind the horns, tore through flesh and bone, shattering its spinal column. The bull dropped where it stood.

Ki replaced the rifle and went to his own horse, and took from his saddlebags the fence pliers that were part of his ranch gear. He snipped the barbwire strands and rode to the pond, leading Sun. Jessie waded out and mounted.

"What about the dead bull?" she asked Ki. "If whatever's wrong with it is contagious, we'd better drag it out of the pasture."

Ki nodded. "We will, but I've got an idea what set it off. We'll take a minute and find out whether I'm right."

After they'd looped their lariats around the dead bull's horns and dragged it outside the fence, Ki patched the strands as best he could. The fence sagged, but it would last for a day or two, until one of the hands could fix it more permanently. Ki took his slim, curved *ko-dachi* from his saddlebags and bent over the dead bull.

11

Jessie followed him, and watched while he slit the animal open. The keen knifeblade quickly opened the bull's belly, and Ki dragged out its intestines, then cut across its gullet to free the four linked stomachs. Dragging out the stomachs, Ki paid no attention to the three small pouches, but cut into the rumen and turned its undigested contents out onto the ground.

"I had an idea this was what we'd find," he said. He lifted a bedraggled length of vegetation on the tip of the *ko-dachi*. "I don't know enough about botany to give it more of a name, but the ranch hands call it locoweed. When cattle eat it, they go crazy."

Jessie frowned. "We got rid of all those weeds years ago, Ki. Alex had the hands dig them out wherever a patch grew."

"I remember. But they're hard to kill."

"I'll tell Ed to have the men find them. I think I've had all the excitement I want today."

★

Chapter 2

By the time Jessie and Ki got back to the ranch house, Ed Wright had returned with the mail. Riding the twenty miles to the little two-store, one-saloon-and-post-office crossroads town was a job the Circle Star foreman reserved as his own responsibility, even though it cost him a day out of every week to make the forty-mile round trip. Wright trusted himself to see that the mail reached Jessie intact, and couldn't quite bring himself to put the same trust in any of the hands.

There was a flour sack full of mail. Jessie dumped it onto the table in the main room of the ranch house and began to sort it out. The sack contained not only her personal mail, but that for the ranch hands. In addition to the letters and postal cards, there were oversized envelopes postmarked New York, Chicago, Washington, New Orleans, Denver, San Francisco, London, Paris, and Tokyo, which contained reports from the various branch offices of the widespread Starbuck enterprises.

Jessie put these aside. All of them had been posted from a week to a month ago, and whatever the reports contained could wait a few more hours before she read them. She winnowed out the few letters and postcards addressed to the ranch hands, and gave them to Wright to deliver. Then she began looking at the remaining mail, a dozen letters addressed to her personally.

"Here's one I'm surprised to see," she told Ki. "From Dave Clemson. The last time I heard from him was just before he got married." She looked at the postmark and frowned. "That's odd. Dave seems to have moved. I hope he's not in trouble."

"He might be wanting his old job back," Ki suggested. "It can't be easy going, starting a ranch in that raw country up in the Panhandle."

"Well, Dave was a very good foreman," Jessie said absently, opening the letter. "But I'm perfectly satisfied with the way Ed's handling things."

At first Jessie read Dave Clemson's letter quickly, scanning each of its three pages of labored script. She was frowning by the time she'd read the second page. When she'd finished the third page, she went back and reread the second. This time she read slowly, and her frown became an expression of thoughtful concern.

Jessie handed the letter to Ki, saying, "Here, Ki. Read this, and then tell me whether I'm imagining things."

Ki took the letter and read it. As Jessie had done, he began to frown when he'd finished the second page, and the frown remained on his face when he lifted his eyes from the pages and looked at Jessie.

"It's not the kind of letter I'd expect Dave to write," he said thoughtfully.

"That's what struck me," she nodded. "Dave never was one to use a lot of words, or to repeat what he'd just said."

"Well, he certainly repeats himself here," Ki agreed.

"Especially those few lines about that area where his new ranch is located." Jessie extended her hand, and Ki returned the letter to her and she reread it. Looking up, she asked, "Did you ever hear of this place called Greer County, Ki?"

"No. Even if it is in Texas—and after reading Dave's letter, I'm not sure it is—it's a long way from the Circle Star," he answered. "And it's not in a part of the country where you have any business interests."

"Denver would be the nearest Starbuck headquarters," Jessie said thoughtfully, as much to herself as to Ki. "Let's go into Alex's study, Ki. I'd like to check my memory against a map."

In contrast to the huge living room of the ranch house, the study seemed almost cozy. The high-ceilinged living room was dominated by the massive slate-gray fieldstone fireplace over which hung the nearly life-sized portrait of the mother Jessie had never seen. All the furniture was in a scale that matched the room's dimensions. Grouped on the floor of wide polished oak planks were several tables holding kerosene lamps that cast a warm glow over the two leather-upholstered sofas and several matching chairs, all the chairs wide enough to allow two people to sit in them comfortably.

Alex's study—Jessie never thought of it in any other terms; the room was still her father's, even though she used it now—was furnished luxuriously, though spartanly. One wall was lined with bookshelves, all well-filled, and in addition to a seldom-used fireplace, the room held a small baseburner with isinglass set in the pierced grill of the door. There were a three-place divan, two chairs upholstered in matching leather, and along one wall the scarred old rolltop oak desk that had been the first piece of furniture bought by Alex when he set up his initial business venture in San Francisco.

Jessie went to the bookshelves and took out an atlas while Ki settled into one of the armchairs. Jessie carried the atlas to the divan and laid it on the seat, snuggling down beside it. She never sat on that particular sofa without seeming to get a faint whiff of the familiar aroma of the pungent cherry-flavored pipe tobacco Alex Starbuck had used.

Opening the atlas to a double-fold map of the United States, she measured distances with her thumbnail. Looking up at Ki, she said, "Greer County's a little over three hundred miles from here. And it's over four hundred miles from there to Denver. The place is also off the beaten track. The map doesn't show any towns in it, and no railroads run through it. No wonder we don't know much about it."

"Just how did Dave describe Greer County?" Ki asked her. "'Disputed territory,' wasn't that how he put it?" After a moment's thought he added, "That could mean a lot of things, depending on who's doing the disputing."

Jessie nodded. "I didn't quite understand what he meant until I'd read his letter the second time. But unless I'm wrong, Texas claims Greer County, but the United States insists it's included in the land given the Indians when they were resettled in the Indian Territory."

"That's the land Dave said is between two forks of the Red River. Does the river show on that map you have, Jessie?"

After glancing at the map, Jessie shook her head, then turned pages in the atlas until she found a map of the Indian Territory. She studied it for a moment and looked up.

"I can see how a dispute like that could develop, Ki," she said. "I remember learning when I studied geography that the Red River is the northern boundary of Texas. But his map shows a fork of the Red River about, oh, a good hundred miles to the north of the Texas state line on this map. From what Dave says in his letter, Texas says that northern fork is really the main river and claims all the land south of it."

"And as long as there's a dispute, with nobody able to prove who the county belongs to, anybody can go into it and fence off as much land as he's able, and neither Texas nor the United States really has any right to stop him," Ki said thoughtfully.

"That's what Dave seems to have done," Jessie nodded. "If you remember, he says in this letter that no homestead limitations are being enforced up there."

"That's not what really caught my eye, though," Ki put in. "I was interested in the part about others taking advantage of the loophole in the law. I'm sure you noticed it too."

"Yes." After a brief pause she went on, "We both know Dave Clemson's a careful man, Ki. He didn't want to put anything in a letter that might get lost in the mails, or that someone might intercept and read."

"That's why he went into so much detail, trying to give us a hint without putting his real meaning into words." Ki referred to the letter again before asking, "Did this letter give you the idea I have, Jessie?"

"I'm sure we're thinking the same thing," she replied. "In a place where there isn't any law, the cartel would certainly be able to set up a base of operations a lot closer to the Circle Star than any they have now."

"We've never been able to touch their New Orleans headquarters," Ki frowned. "But it's too far away to operate very effectively against the Circle Star. That's one reason things have been fairly peaceful here."

"Distances are shrinking, even in Texas," Jessie thought aloud. "Railroads are wiping them out. It's hard to realize, but now that the Southern Pacific has taken over the Texas & Pacific, we're only a two-day ride to railhead, Ki. If the cartel should get a headquarters in Texas, they could strike here whenever they wanted to." Her jaw set, she faced Ki. "You know how I feel about the ranch. It's the one peaceful place I know, the one

17

place where I feel safe and happy. I don't want to see it turned into a battlefield."

"No. Once was enough," Ki said. His voice was usually level and unperturbed even under the greatest stress, but now it was harsh and bitter.

For a moment Ki's mood communicated itself to Jessie, and she fell silent too. Then she picked up Dave Clemson's letter and turned to the last page.

"Tell me how you'd translate this, Ki. You remember how Dave hated to write letters, and how he tried to make them as short as possible." Jessie found the place in the letter and read, "'I don't know if you're planning to take a trip anytime soon, Jessie, but if you should just happen to travel up this way, be sure to drop in and see us.'" Raising her eyes from the letter, she asked, "If you take out the extra words Dave's put in, Ki, what is he really saying?"

Ki thought for a moment, then said, "Something like this: 'Take a trip soon, Jessie, travel up here and see me.'"

"That's how I read it too," Jessie agreed. "That's why he gave such careful directions to his new ranch, so we could find it without any trouble. I think I could get there without even looking at a map."

"We're going to Greer County, then?"

"Of course."

"I was sure we would, five minutes ago." Ki smiled. "When?"

"As soon as we can leave, I suppose. There are still a few things I need to talk about with Ed. Day after tomorrow?"

"If it suits you," Ki nodded.

"Good. And let's take our own horses this time, Ki. After riding Sun, I'd be unhappy riding a rented horse from a livery stable. We'll ride them up to the railhead, and the stationmaster will make space in the baggage car for the horses. He's done it before, you know."

"He should," Ki said. "Considering the number of cattle cars the Circle Star uses every roundup." He stood up and went over to the divan, picked up the atlas, and found the map Jessie had been using. After studying it for a few moments, he said, "It looks like Wichita Falls is the best place to start from."

"I think so too. And I always enjoy the overnight layover in San Antonio."

"Then we'll ship the horses through to Wichita Falls. If this map's accurate, it's not more than a two-day ride from there to the place where Dave's new ranch is."

As Ki stepped over to replace the atlas on the bookshelves, Jessie looked around the familiar room. She said, "I was hoping we'd be able to stay here for a while, this time. But if we've read Dave's letter right, there's something going on up there where he is that could threaten the Circle Star."

"Since both of us got the same idea, I don't see how we could be wrong, Jessie."

Again, Jessie set her jaw determinedly. She told Ki, "You know how I feel about this place, Ki. Rest isn't as important as making sure it's not going to be disturbed again. To keep it peaceful, we've got to be willing to fight!"

"I can't understand why progress always leaves such ugly scars behind it," Jessie remarked as she and Ki stood on the platform of the flagstop station two days later, waiting for the eastbound train. "It's been two years now since this was the T&P railhead, but it still looks more like a battlefield than a railroad depot."

Ki surveyed the jumble of rusted rails, snarled and ragged ends of steel cable, cracked and discarded wheels of railway cars and wagons, and broken ties scattered across the rutted and beaten earth that surrounded the depot on both sides of the track.

"I suppose it'll get cleaned up someday," he said. "But Alex was certainly right when he refused to sell the railroad any right-of-way through Circle Star range."

"He was a wise man," Jessie said. "And a good one. That's why the cartel had him murdered."

A distant whistle interrupted Ki as he was about to reply. He and Jessie looked into the declining sun and watched while the train rounded the curve and entered the long, straight stretch of rails that led into the station. The stationmaster came out of the little tan-and-brown-painted depot and pulled a baggage cart up to the center of the platform.

"There's a shipment for your ranch that will have to be unloaded before your horses can be put in the baggage car, Miss Starbuck," he said. "But it'll only take a few minutes. I've already wired down the line to the last station stop for them to make room for the critters."

"Thank you," Jessie nodded. "My foreman's expecting the shipment, I know. He'll send some of the hands with a wagon to pick it up in a few days."

Jessie was conscious of the man's admiring glances, but paid no attention to them. In spite of the fact that she and Ki had left the Circle Star long before sunup to reach the station by noon, she looked as fresh as though she'd just bathed and dressed.

She was dressed in her favorite travel costume: a green tweed riding skirt with a matching jacket, over a cream-colored silk blouse. Her brown Stetson dangled down her back by its chin-thong, leaving her blonde hair to ripple in the light breeze. Low-heeled boots of cordovan leather were on her feet. Since the first leg of their journey would be safely routine, she'd packed her gunbelt and Colt in her saddlebags, but in her jacket pocket she carried the little double-barreled derringer with ivory grips that served as her backup weapon.

Ki, in contrast, had on the same leather vest and cotton shirt and denims that he wore at the ranch, and the same rope-soled slippers with tops of black cotton duck. Like Jessie he was apparently unarmed, but in the pockets of his vest he had his usual supply of deadly *shuriken,* and as usual when he traveled, Ki's razor-edged *ko-dachi,* in its sheath, was tucked into the innocent-looking woven horsehair *surushin* which he wore as a belt.

It suited both his and Jessie's purposes when they traveled among strangers for Ki to appear to be her servant rather than her trusted companion. Many times in the past, the tendency of agents of the cartel to ignore Ki as an inconsequential attendant had gotten both him and Jessie out of tight spots.

With a squealing of steel brake shoes on steel wheels and an expiring gush of steam, the train come to a stop. The door of the baggage car was centered on the platform, the passenger coaches behind it. The conductor swung out of the first coach and placed the passenger step-stool on the ground.

"You might as well go on and get aboard, Jessie," Ki suggested. "I'll see that the horses are loaded."

"You're sure you won't change your mind about riding in the coach with me?" Jessie asked.

Ki shook his head. "The horses can't look out for themselves the way you can, Jessie, and they're not really used to traveling on a train. Besides, I like to keep an eye on our gear to be sure it's not disturbed."

Though Jessie and Ki were traveling light, their saddle gear made a sizable heap on the platform. In addition to their saddles and saddlebags, rifles and bedrolls, there was the packsaddle and its panniers filled with supplies,

21

which would be carried by the packhorse they were taking in addition to their mounts. Jessie looked at the piled-up equipment and nodded.

"You're right, of course. And it's not a very long trip to San Antonio. We should get there shortly after dark."

Already the stationmaster was wheeling the crate-laden cart out of the baggage car. He nodded to Jessie and Ki and said, "If you're ready, we can load your horses now, Miss Starbuck."

With a farewell nod to Jessie, Ki dropped off the side of the platform where the palomino and roan were teth-ered. Jessie walked along the edge of the roadbed to the passenger coach, and was handed up the step by the conductor. She'd barely gotten into the coach and found a seat at the rear when the train began to roll forward. Once settled, Jessie looked toward the front of the coach to take stock of her fellow passengers.

Like most of the railroads of the day, the Southern Pacific had few eastbound customers, but the tidal wave of emigrants looking for land of their own on the vast and fertile expanses between the Mississippi and the Pacific crowded the trains going west. There were only five other passengers in the coach: an elderly couple in seats near the center, a woman with a young child across from them, and a man in one of the forward seats. Jessie could see nothing except the backs of their heads until the man stood up and started down the aisle to the back.

To Jessie's surprise, he stopped beside her seat and took off his gray derby hat. "Miss Starbuck," he said, his tone a half-question, "I don't know whether you re-member me, but we've met before. I'm Greg Hendricks. I was on the Texas & Pacific legal staff when we were trying to negotiate with your father for a right-of-way across the Circle Star ranch."

"I remember attending some meetings with my father,"

Jessie said. "But that was a number of years ago, and a great deal has happened since then."

Hendricks nodded. "I heard of Mr. Starbuck's tragic death. Are you still living on the ranch, or do you just visit it now and then?"

"Oh, I still look on it as home," Jessie replied.

She had been studying Hendricks without seeming to do so. The attorney looked to be in his early thirties. He was clean-shaven, his face just beginning to show lines of maturity. His hair was dark, his face square, with a determined jut to his jaw. His gray eyes were clear and met hers without hesitation. Under an aquiline nose, his lips were full and well formed. He had the air of self-confidence that comes with success earned through individual effort.

"I don't mean to intrude on you, if you'd rather sit alone," he said. "But quite frankly, I'm bored after having ridden on this train for the past three days. I'd be grateful if we could just sit together and chat on the way to San Antonio."

There was something about his straightforward approach that struck a responsive chord in Jessie. She smiled and indicated the seat beside her. "Sit down, Mr. Hendricks," she said. "I think I'd rather talk with you than sit by myself and get as bored as you say you are."

★

Chapter 3

Hendricks put his derby on the rack above the seat before sitting down next to Jessie. He said, "If you get sleepy or bored, Miss Starbuck, don't be bashful about letting me know. I certainly wouldn't want to intrude on your privacy."

"You're not," Jessie assured him. "You mentioned that when we met before, you were on the T&P legal staff. Are you still working for them?"

Hendricks shook his head. "After the Southern Pacific forced Mr. Scott into a corner and took control of the road, they had all the lawyers they needed in their own legal department, and I found myself out of a job. I was reasonably well known in St. Louis by that time, so I was offered a partnership in a very good firm. I'm on my way back home now after handling a claims case against the SP in San Francisco."

"I'm sure your wife will be glad to see you."

"Oh, I'm not married, Miss Starbuck. I don't even have any prospects."

Jessie looked at the young attorney and smiled. "Since we're going to be sharing a seat to San Antonio, why don't we stop being formal? My friends call me Jessie."

"Thank you, Jessie. And I answer best to Greg."

"Good. What do you do when you're not in court, Greg?"

"Well, St. Louis doesn't offer much in the way of outdoor activity. My work with the T&P kept me in Texas a good part of the time, and I got used to riding across open country. When I went back to riding on a bridle path in a city, I found it too tame to be interesting, so I joined an athletic club. Now I swim a lot, play a little tennis, and at least twice a week I fence, usually with the epee."

"Fencing's always fascinated me," Jessie said. "It's both delicate and deadly. It's too bad it's a man's sport."

"It isn't anymore. There are two women's fencing clubs in St. Louis now, and I understand the sport's become very popular among ladies in New York and Boston."

"Someday I'd like to try it," Jessie said. "Not that it would do me any good on the Circle Star. When someone talks about fencing in this part of the country, they mean barbwire."

Jessie and Greg Hendricks chatted through the long afternoon, spurts of conversation broken by companionable silence, as the train rolled east. There were few station stops as the rails ran through the sparsely grassed flatlands that stretched southwest from the Edwards Plateau. When they reached the beginning of the river-rich coastal plains, and rangeland gave way to farms, the distances between towns grew shorter, the stops more frequent, and passengers began to fill the coach. The bright sunshine faded into twilight, then to dusk. The train slowed appreciably, and Hendricks looked past Jessie, out of the window.

"We're pulling into San Antonio, Jessie," he said. "Since we both have a layover there until morning, I hope you'll accept an invitation to have dinner with me."

Jessie hesitated momentarily. "I'd enjoy that, Greg,

but I have someone traveling with me. Ki's in the baggage coach, keeping an eye on our gear and our horses."

"Ki?" Hendricks frowned.

"Yes. That's his full name. It's not a nickname, the way Greg is short for Gregory."

"Your manservant, I suppose?"

"No. Ki was my father's companion, now he's mine. I don't consider him a servant in any way."

"I see," Hendricks said, though it was obvious that he didn't. "In that case, I'll include him in my invitation."

"I can't accept for Ki," Jessie replied. "He isn't obliged to have meals with me, and he may have some plans of his own. If he does, then I'll be delighted to have dinner with you, Greg."

"You'll be staying at the Menger, of course?"

Jessie nodded. "Father kept a suite there for many years, and I grew so used to the hotel that I never think of going anywhere else."

"You'll be kept busy looking after your horses and gear when we reach the depot," Hendricks said. "Suppose I find out your room number from the desk clerk, and rap on your door about eight o'clock? And I assure you, I'll be delighted to have both you and your companion as my guests for dinner, if—Ki, isn't it?—decides to join us."

"That'll be fine," Jessie agreed. "I'll be ready."

In the hackney cab on their way to the hotel, after they'd arranged for the horses to be stabled overnight at the railroad yards, Jessie told Ki of the tentative arrangement she'd agreed to for their dinner.

Ki looked at her quizzically for a moment, then shook his head. "I wouldn't think of intruding on a dinner with you and your new friend."

"Greg's a very personable man, Ki. And a gentleman. I'm sure he's sincere when he says you'll be welcome."

"No, Jessie. I'm afraid it would make things awkward. Anyway, the real reason I'm saying no is that I've been thinking for the past fifty miles about what I'd like to do this evening."

"And what is that?"

"After I wash off the soot and cinders, I intend to stretch my legs with a walk down Commerce Street to Haymarket Plaza. I'll buy a bottle of Pearl Beer at the saloon on the corner there, and then take my time strolling around the plaza enjoying the real Mexican food the chili queens cook."

"Of course. I should have remembered how much you like to eat while you walk around down there."

"Our train to Wichita Falls leaves at eight-thirty in the morning," Ki reminded Jessie.

"We'd better meet in the lobby for breakfast about seven, then," Jessie said. "And you can arrange with the doorman to have a hack waiting to take us to the depot."

Ki looked out as the hackman turned the carriage into the porte-cochere at the side of the Menger Hotel and pulled up.

"That should give us plenty of time," he said.

With a flourish the doorman opened the carriage door and bowed Jessie and Ki into the cool, quiet lobby of the low, rambling, cut-limestone building. They crossed the polished flagstone floor to the reception desk.

"Why, Miss Starbuck!" the desk clerk said as he looked up from the register. "It's a pleasure to welcome you back to the Menger. You haven't visited us for quite some time. And Mr. Ki! It's good to see you again too." He looked at Jessie again. "If you'd like Mr. Starbuck's old suite—"

"No," Jessie interrupted. On the train she'd decided that even if the suite should be vacant, she'd refuse it, for it held too many memories of the past. She signed

27

the register and moved aside for Ki to sign. "No, we're only stopping between trains. Single rooms will be quite all right."

"Certainly." The clerk tapped his call-bell twice, and a pair of bellboys materialized. "I'm sure you'll find the rooms satisfactory, Miss Starbuck. If they aren't, we'll be glad to change them, of course."

In her room, Jessie enjoyed a leisurely bath, and as she dressed again, she half regretted that she hadn't brought along any city clothes. Then she shrugged, arranged her hair, and was just sitting down to wait for Hendricks to knock when there was a light tapping on the door.

"I hope I'm not too early," Hendricks greeted her when she opened the door.

"You're just in time," Jessie assured him.

"Will there be three of us at dinner?"

"No. Ki has an appetite for Mexican food that he likes to satisfy when we get to San Antonio."

"Well, since you've already accepted for yourself, suppose we go, then. I'm sure you're as hungry as I am, after that long train ride."

"To tell you the truth, Greg, I'm hungry enough right now to eat almost anything."

"Does German food appeal to you?" he asked as they walked down the long corridor toward the lobby.

"It appeals to me very much," Jessie replied, taking Hendricks's arm as they left the hotel and started down Crockett Street. "I haven't tasted any German cooking for so long it'll be a treat."

"There's a place called Schilto's just a few steps from here," Greg said, taking her arm as they turned into Alamo Plaza. "It isn't fancy. In fact, it's a beer garden behind a saloon. But the food is excellent, and I thought you might enjoy something besides the regular steaks and roasts that are served almost universally."

"I'm sure I will," Jessie told him.

They crossed the plaza, getting a glimpse of the ghostly white stone walls of the ruined Alamo, standing roofless and deserted in the light of the gas streetlamps.

On the west side of the plaza, stores and business buildings predominated; Jessie and Greg walked along, enjoying the cool evening breeze and glancing into the stores, most of them still open for businesss, though there were few pedestrians on the street. Greg took Jessie's arm again as they reached Commerce Street and turned in the direction of the narrow iron suspension bridge that spanned the little San Antonio River, its shallow waters black now in the night. Across the bridge, the swinging doors of a saloon flopped and a patron came out, walking a bit unsteadily.

"That's Schilto's Saloon," Greg said, "but we don't have to go through it to get to the beer garden. We'll just walk on to the corner and turn left."

Behind the saloon, awnings had been erected to cover a large area. Lanterns were hung from the supporting posts, and glowed cheerfully on tables spread with red-checked cloths. Perhaps a dozen of the thirty or so tables were occupied, most of them by family groups. Aproned waiters, balancing huge trays, made their way along the aisles between the tables.

"I warned you that we weren't going to a deluxe cafe," Greg said as he guided Jessie to a table. "But it's a lot more relaxing after a day on the train than the Menger dining room, which I find just a little bit stuffy."

"I think it's very nice," Jessie replied. "But you'll have to order for me, because I don't know a thing about German food."

"We'll try for something different," he replied. "But tell me whether you'd prefer wine or beer with dinner."

"Wine, I think," Jessie said. "Something cool and light."

"Most German wines are. But I think you'll enjoy what I have in mind."

They sat down at a vacant table, and Greg ordered without looking at the menu offered by the waiter. Within a few moments the waiter was back, carrying stemmed glasses and a napkin-wrapped bottle. He went through the formality of pouring a small amount of wine in Greg's glass and getting a nod of approval before filling Jessie's glass, then Greg's. Jessie sipped the wine. It was cool and slightly tart, refreshing on a summer night.

"Oh, this is very good," she said. "I'd like to order some for the ranch. What is it, Greg?"

"A Kieselberg Reisling, just about right for the main course I've ordered."

"Would you like to tell me about it, or should I wait and be surprised?"

"We're having a dish called Schemmerolle, and even if the name sounds fancy, it's nothing but thin slices of beefsteak rolled around a stuffing of ground pork and veal, simmered in a cream sauce. The seasoning is what counts, and I'm not too sure I remember all the herbs and spices that go into it. But it's something of a specialty here, and I hope you'll like it."

"It sounds wonderful, and I'm sure I'll enjoy it. And the waiter can't serve us too soon, because I'm as hungry as a bear."

Jessie did indeed enjoy the beef roulades, and after she and Greg had eaten until their appetites were satisfied, they lingered at the table, comparing foods they enjoyed, talking of the differences in cities with which they were both familiar, of ranch life as contrasted to that in the legal profession.

Each time Greg began to steer the conversation to a more personal level, Jessie carefully brought it back to one of impersonal friendliness. Though she was attracted

30

to the young attorney, she had not yet made up her mind about Greg Hendricks. While they talked, the tables around them emptied one by one, until Jessie looked around and saw that they had the beer garden to themselves.

"In case you haven't noticed, Greg," she said, "we're the only ones left here, and it must be long past time for this place to close."

"Oh, I don't think so," Greg replied. "The saloon's open all night, so they wouldn't be in any hurry for us to leave. I was just about to suggest that I order another bottle of wine."

"I've had enough for tonight, thanks. And we both have to think about tomorrow."

"I'd much rather think about extending tonight," Greg replied. "You're a fascinating woman, Jessie. I enjoy being with you. I'll hate to see the evening end."

"I will too," she answered honestly. "But it is late, and we'd better go."

Greg called for a waiter, and while he settled the bill and waited for his change, one of the other waiters appeared and began blowing out the lanterns. To keep from getting in the waiter's way, Jessie walked to the edge of the sheltered area and stood at the sidewalk. She was waiting in the growing gloom for Greg to join her when a uniformed policeman appeared out of the darkness. Jessie stepped back to give the man room to pass, but he stopped in front of her and looked at her narrowly.

"Is something wrong, officer?" she asked.

"Is your name Jessica Starbuck?" he asked, his thick brows drawn together in the beginning of a frown.

"Yes, it is. Why?"

Jessie's surprise was so total that she did not react with her usual speed. Before she realized his intention, the policeman slid a pair of handcuffs from his belt and

31

snapped them around her wrists.

"You'll have to come along with me, Miss Starbuck," he said. "You're under arrest."

"Why? What have I done?"

Before the man could answer, Greg walked up. He took in the scene at a glance and asked, "What's wrong, Jessie? Why has this officer handcuffed you?"

"I've no more idea than you have, Greg," Jessie replied. "He asked my name, and when I told him, he handcuffed me before I knew what was happening."

Greg turned to the policeman, "Officer, do you know who Miss Starbuck is?" he asked angrily.

"I don't care who she is," the man snapped. "She's told me her name, and I've got orders to bring her in."

"That's preposterous!" Greg said angrily. "What's Miss Starbuck charged with?"

"Now that's no affair of yours, mister," the uniformed man replied. "This is police business, and if you're smart you'll get out of here and stay clear of it."

"Nonsense!" Hendricks snorted. "I'm an attorney, and as of this minute I'm representing Miss Starbuck. Now, either tell me the reason you've arrested her, or take your handcuffs off her!"

Instead of replying, the policeman whipped a blackjack from his sleeve and swung it in a sideswiping blow that caught Greg behind the ear. The attorney crumpled soundlessly to the ground.

Jessie began to struggle then, but the burly policeman clamped one arm around her, lifted her off the ground, then sealed her mouth with his other hand before she could loose the scream she was forming. He whistled, his lips so close to Jessie's ear that the shrill sound almost deafened her.

Hoofbeats and the crunch of carriage wheels sounded from the darkness, and in a moment a four-wheeled carriage drew up to where the policeman stood.

She stopped struggling, to conserve her strength for a later time when her chances for escape might be better, and used her eyes and ears to the best advantage. Even in the dark she could see well enough to tell that the man on the carriage seat, like the bogus policeman, was one she'd never seen before.

"Get that rag and tie her mouth up," the bogus cop said to the man on the carriage seat. "And we'll get her in the hack. We better take this dude I knocked out, too. If we leave him here, he'll have the cops after us before we can get clear."

"Wait a minute now!" the carriage driver protested. "The boss didn't say we was to bring anybody but the woman."

"*I'm* the boss as far as you're concerned right now!" the policeman snapped. "Hurry up with that rag, so we can keep this woman quiet. It's going to take both of us to load the man in."

"All right, all right!" the second man grumbled. "But the boss ain't gonna like it one little bit."

Mumbling angrily under his breath, the driver got down and rummaged in the passenger compartment until he found a rag. He stepped back to where the fake cop was holding Jessie, and twisted the rag into a thick cylinder. The phony policeman released her mouth and the second man quickly pulled the cloth between Jessie's lips and knotted it at the back of her neck.

"Now we'll put her in the hack while we pick up the man," the uniformed thug said.

"She'll get away!" the driver objected.

"Not if we work fast, she won't. Damn it, Spud, do what I tell you to! We're wasting too much time! That fellow ain't going to stay out much longer."

Jessie was lifted into the carriage and pushed down on its back seat with a rough shove.

"If you know what's good for you, you'll stay right

33

here," the fake policeman threatened.

Jessie nodded, hoping they could see her in the dark. She had no intention of trying to run. Unless the men searched her, she held the card that would trump their aces, the little derringer in her jacket pocket. Even handcuffed, she had enough play in her arms and hands to get to the gun.

She sat quietly in the carriage while the two men lifted Greg and shoved him into the seat beside her. He was still out, and his body slumped limply against her.

"All right," the phony cop told his companion, "get this damned hack moving. I'll ride inside." He got in the carriage, slammed the door, and settled on the seat facing Jessie and Greg. Pulling his revolver from its holster, he said with quiet menace, "You'll be all right as long as you behave. But don't fool yourself for a minute. I'll shoot both of you if I've got to."

★

Chapter 4

Jessie sat quietly while the carriage moved away. From the moment the man posing as a policeman abandoned his pretense, it had been obvious to her quicksilver mind what was happening. Only the cartel operated in such a style.

She could think of no reason for the unexpected attack, but her experiences with the cartel in the past had taught her that its masters moved in devious ways in their unrelenting efforts to take over the Starbuck industrial empire. She did not waste time trying to deduce the immediate motive for her capture, but turned instead to thinking of a way to escape.

For the moment, there seemed to be none. The carriage was a landau, with facing seats at front and rear. It had windows only in the doors, and both of these had glass-paned openings, but they were blocked by opaque curtains. Even if they had not been, from her position Jessie would have been unable to see outside.

She and Greg had been placed on the rear seat, and the man in policeman's uniform sat on the front seat, facing them. Each time they rolled past a streetlight, the interior was illuminated dimly and briefly when the curtains brightened and flashes of light leaked in through cracks around the edges of the curtains. When this happened, Jessie got fleeting glimpses of her captor as the carriage rumbled over the brick-paved streets. Each time she saw that he was holding his revolver steadily, aimed at her.

On the seat beside her, Greg stirred and groaned. The landau had left the downtown area by now, in a series of sharp turns that quickly took it to unlighted streets. Jessie's eyes adjusted quickly as the darkness inside the vehicle grew deeper. She could still see the dim outline of the fake police officer sitting across from them, his revolver ready. Greg stirred again and sat up.

"What the hell—" he began.

"Shut up!" their uniformed captor commanded harshly. "You make a nuisance out of yourself, I'll put a bullet through you. We don't have to take you along, all we need is the woman."

"I want to know what this is all about," Greg said, his voice stronger now, and angry.

"And I won't tell you no more to keep your face shut!" the phony cop snapped. "You say one more word and you're dead!"

With the gag in her mouth, Jessie could not tell Greg to keep quiet, but she did the next best thing. Her legs were free, and she slid her foot along the floor until she felt Greg's foot, and pressed on it with hers. Greg turned to look at her, and she shook her head, hoping that he'd grasp her message. He opened his mouth instinctively before catching the meaning of Jessie's signal, then he swallowed hard and fell quiet.

For what seemed a very long time, the carriage kept moving. From the sound of its wheels, Jessie could deduce that she and Greg were being taken to the outskirts of San Antonio, and perhaps even farther into the countryside.

At first the wheels rumbled over the brick pavement,

but soon the rumbling changed to a grating as the pavement gave way to gravel, then the noise of the wheels grew almost inaudible as even gravel-paved streets were left behind and the carriage moved with gentle lurchings over what Jessie decided must be dirt lanes. Then it creaked to a stop, and she could hear the man on the seat crawling down. The carriage door opened, and she got a glimpse of a small, shabby house outside.

"How you wanta get 'em inside, Beggs?" the driver asked. "We can take 'em both in at once, or one at a time."

"They won't give us no trouble, Spud," the uniformed man replied. "You open the house and light a lamp. Leave the door open and cover 'em while they get out. If they try to run, you shoot the woman, I'll take the man."

Jessie abandoned her half-formed plan for an immediate escape. With the man called Spud in front of them and Beggs behind them, and her wrists hampered by the heavy handcuffs, she knew she could not get her derringer from her pocket and drop both of them fast enough to keep one of the two from firing.

Inside the house, a match flared. The flare settled down to a steady yellow glow through the opened door. Spud came out, a pistol in his hand now. He said, "All right, whenever you say."

"You heard what I said to Spud," Beggs told Jessie and Greg, his voice harsh. He jerked his pistol at Jessie. "Now you get out and walk in the door. And you"—his gun muzzle turned to Greg—"you go right after her. Just don't forget for a minute that I'm in back of you with this gun."

"I'm not anxious to get myself killed," Greg answered.

He crawled out of the landau. Beggs motioned with the gun's barrel for Jessie to follow. She did so, and

Beggs followed her into the house. The room they entered was small and bare of furniture, except for two chairs and a table. Above the table a kerosene lamp hung from the ceiling, still swaying from having been handled when Spud lighted it. The air was stale and smelled heavily of tobacco smoke.

Jessie glanced around quickly, seeking possibilities for escape. A narrow hall opened at the back of the room, flanked by doors on either side. The room had windows on both sides and other windows flanking the door. All the windows were shuttered; Jessie could see the slats of the wooden shutters through the windowpanes. Beggs closed the door behind him. Jessie had seen nothing helpful in the room, and gave her attention to Spud. She'd seen enough of Beggs when he made his fake arrest to be able to describe him, but this was the first good look she'd gotten at the other man.

Spud was as different from Beggs as it was possible to be. He was wiry and spare, where Beggs was tall and beefy. Spud had a long, thin nose and a sharp chin; a straggly mustache adorned his wizened, tanned face. Beggs's face was round and clean-shaven, his nose a small button and his chin a knob; his complexion was choleric. The one thing the two men had in common was the icy stare that marks the merciless killer.

Beggs told Spud, "We got maybe an hour to wait. The boss said he won't be here till after midnight, and there ain't much use in us setting around that long, holding our guns on these two. I guess we better lock 'em up till he gets here."

Spud walked across the room and opened one of the doors. He said, "All right. You two go on in here."

"Wait a minute," Beggs said. "Put the Starbuck dame in one room and the man in the other one. That way they can't pull no surprises on us."

"Good idea," Spud agreed.

38

He started toward Jessie. She turned to Beggs, raised her handcuffed hands, and fingered the roll of cloth in her mouth.

Greg said, "Miss Starbuck wants you to take the gag off."

At Greg's first words, both Beggs and Spud swiveled their weapons to cover him. Jessie took advantage of her momentary freedom from observation by looking at Greg and shaking her head, hoping he'd get her message to stay silent. He did. His mouth had been open to continue protesting, but he closed it quickly.

Beggs grated, "I told you to keep quiet!" Then he turned back to Spud and said, "Ah, hell, you might as well take her gag off. She'd work free of it anyways, soon as she's in the room. Leave them cuffs on her, though. The boss said she's slick as a wet eel."

Spud untied the knot and removed the gag. He warned Jessie, "Now you just better keep real quiet, because there ain't nobody close enough to this place to hear you, even if you was to yell your heads off."

Jessie did not reply. She was working her jaws to relieve their stiffness. She allowed Spud to push her through the door and close it behind her. She heard the scraping of the doorkey as Spud locked the door. She was in darkness again, and while her eyes were adjusting to the gloom, she pressed her ear to the door panel and listened to what was being said in the main room. Beggs's voice came to her faintly.

"You're sure we hadn't better tie 'em up?" Spud asked.

"Hell, yes, I'm sure! The window shutters in them rooms is nailed closed. Nobody seen us take 'em, and they won't be fools enough to jump us. We got the only guns, ain't we?"

"Yeah. I guess they'll be all right." Spud paused, then asked, "Why in hell did the boss want us to take them two the way we did, Beggs, in such a hell of a hurry?"

"Damned if I know. He rousted me out not much more'n an hour ago and said we was to do a hurry-up job. Brought me this damn copper's outfit, told me just how to go about things. Said we was to take the woman by herself if we could, but if we had to take the man, to go ahead and do it."

"Well, I guess he had his reasons," Spud said. "As long as he keeps paying us the way he does, I won't ask questions."

"It's better not to," the big man told him. Then he went on, "Get them cards outta the table drawer. We might as well play some pitch while we're waiting."

Jessie heard the scraping of chair legs on the floor as the two thugs sat down. There was little to be gained by eavesdropping further, she decided. She turned her attention to exploring the room.

Except for a bed, it was bare. She went to the window and looked out, but all she could see was a series of parallel lines where the lesser gloom of the night outside outlined the louvers of the shutters. The conversation she'd overheard between Beggs and Spud only reinforced her certainty that the cartel was responsible for her and Greg being captured, but she could still think of no reason why.

Turning away, she went to the bed and stretched out to think. She could see only one course of action. When the mysterious individual that Beggs and Spud called "the boss" arrived, and the door of the room was opened, she'd have her derringer hidden in her clasped hands. The odds were in her favor that only one of the men would have a gun drawn and ready. He'd be her first target; then, with the single shot left in the derringer, she should be able to immobilize the other two long enough to get her hands on the weapon of the man she'd shot. After that—

Pursing her lips, Jessie shook her head. The plan left

too many things to chance. If both men had guns, she'd have to shoot twice, leaving her with an empty gun, and "the boss" was certain to be armed. With a sigh, Jessie began to reshape her original plan.

She'd just begun mulling over alternative moves when she heard a faint scratching at the window. Taking the derringer from her jacket pocket, clumsily because of the handcuffs on her wrists, she went to the window. The thin slits of light between the louvers were moving when she reached it. They opened fully, and she found herself looking into Ki's familiar face.

Jessie felt a surge of relief. She held a finger to her lips and Ki nodded his understanding of the need for silence. He began to work at the shutter frames, his fingers exploring them, feeling through the gaps between the louvers. He gestured with satisfaction after a moment, then his muscular hands closed on the frames and he began to work the shutters back and forth.

They gave way to his manipulations, slowly but silently. The only noise Jessie heard was a squeaking no louder than a mouse's cry as the nails holding the shutters to the windowframe were pulled from the wood. Still grasping the derringer in one hand, she felt along the inside of the sash until she found the window latch and swiveled it open. By the time Ki placed the shutters on the ground, she was lifting the sash. With the shutters removed, the gloom inside the room lessened perceptibly and fresh night air rushed through the opening. Ki slithered on his belly through the window.

There was no need for them to talk. They'd worked their way together out of so many tight scrapes before that the silent communication between them was almost telepathic.

Ki took Jessie's handcuffed wrists and brought them close to his face. He peered at the cuffs briefly and shook his head.

41

Jessie shrugged, and when Ki released her hands, she pointed to the door and shook her head in warning.

Ki nodded and made a twisting movement with his hand, pointing to the doorknob.

Jessie answered his nod with one of her own.

Ki held up two fingers, his almond eyes questioning.

Jessie held the derringer up, two fingers of her free hand raised, and pointed to the door.

Again Ki signaled his understanding with a small, quick nod. He slid a *shuriken* from his vest pocket and held it up.

Jessie thought for a split second. She held up two fingers, waggling the derringer in her other hand. She closed one finger, drew her hands across her chest, and shook her head.

Ki nodded with a quick jerk of his head. He put one hand on his shoulder, indicated the door, and thrust his body sideways.

Jessie reached a quick decision and nodded for the last time. Without a word having been spoken, their plan of attack was complete.

Jessie tiptoed silently to the door and stood beside it. As soon as she was in place, Ki moved. He thrust his well-schooled leg muscles with all the power he could muster. His shoulder hit the door and its panels splintered. The doorjamb gave way and the door toppled into the main room. His impetus carried Ki into the room, staggering a bit as he fought for balance.

Jessie stepped into the open doorframe. Beggs and Spud sat at the table; a revolver was lying in front of Beggs. Spud had a deck of cards in one hand and a single card in the other.

Beggs had barely closed his hand around the gun on the table when the slug from Jessie's derringer slammed into his chest. The half-grasped pistol slid from his hand as he toppled out of his chair, his falling body hitting the table and overturning it.

Spud had let the cards he was holding drop to the table as he leaped to his feet with the sound of the door being broken down. He was turning toward the sound, clawing at his holster, but before he could draw, Ki had regained his balance. With a backhanded flip of his wrist, he threw the *shuriken*. The thin star-shaped weapon cut into Spud's right shoulder. Spud's gun hand sagged useless to his side.

By then Ki was upon him. His hand darted to Spud's throat and his agile fingers, hard as steel claws, caught the small man's Adam's apple. Ki applied pressure. Spud gasped and wheezed for a moment, then the stabbing tips of Ki's fingers and thumb on the plexus of nerves in the column of Spud's neck took effect. Spud's eyelids fluttered as his eyes turned upward and he went limp.

As Ki released Spud, Greg began pounding on the door of the room where he'd been placed. Ignoring the pounding, Ki let Spud slide to the floor and said to Jessie, "He'll be out for ten minutes or so, but he's not dead. You did signal that you wanted to take one of them alive, didn't you?"

"Yes." Jessie was straightening up after having bent over Beggs to make sure her shot had been true. She started for the door of the second room, where Greg's thumping on the panels had increased in volume. "It didn't matter which one. Judging from the little I overheard, both of them were just hired thugs. Neither one of them knew anything." She unlocked the door and opened it. Greg rushed out.

"What the hell's happening—" He stopped short, his eyes widening at the sight of Beggs and Spud on the floor. "Excuse me, Jessie. I don't usually swear in front of ladies."

"I know. It's all right," she said. "Ki found us, somehow. I haven't had time to ask him how."

"But this . . ." Greg gestured toward the bodies on the floor. "How did you—"

Jessie held up the derringer. "They forgot to search me. I suppose they're not used to anything but city ladies who don't carry guns."

Ki said, "I was on my way back to the Menger when I saw the man in the uniform talking to you two. There was something about the situation that looked wrong, so I stopped to watch. I followed the carriage on foot, but it got ahead of me, and I lost a little time finding it. I didn't want to make a premature move, so I waited until they'd settled down and were off guard."

Greg's face showed his bewilderment. He gulped, then said very slowly, "You act like this kind of thing happens to you all the time."

"It isn't that bad, Greg," Jessie assured him. "And you'd have trouble understanding unless I told you the whole story."

Greg looked at her searchingly. "This is connected with your father's death somehow, isn't it, Jessie?"

"Yes. But there's not enough time for me to explain now. If you were listening at your door the way I was, you know that whoever hired these two will be here soon."

"You hadn't mentioned that," Ki said.

"I couldn't think of a way to signal it to you, Ki. The only thing I wanted to do was to get out of that room as quickly as possible. But if we rearrange this room to look normal, we might get answers to a lot of things we can only guess at now."

Greg shook his head. "You're talking about something I still don't understand, but I'm sure you wouldn't be involved in anything at all shady, Jessie. What can I do to help?"

"We've got to capture the man who hired these two," Jessie replied. "I didn't make any plans beyond trying to get away, and Ki changed those."

Before Jessie stopped speaking, Ki was in motion. He righted the fallen table and the chair that Spud had kicked aside as he jumped up. He asked Greg, "Can you use a pistol?"

"Fairly well. I'm not—"

"Never mind how good or bad a shot you are, Greg," Jessie said. Ki was putting the room in order, and she began helping him. She picked up Beggs's gun from the floor and handed it to Greg. "Put this in your belt and use it if you have to. Now let's fix this room so it looks undisturbed to someone coming in the front door. We'll put the big man in the chair facing the door. Ki, you open the door and stay behind it so whoever comes in won't see you. Greg, we'll put the live one in the room you were in and you can keep an eye on him. How much longer will he stay unconscious, Ki?"

"It's hard to say. But he won't be able to put up much of a fight when he comes around."

"Take him to the room, then," Jessie said. "Greg and I will finish fixing things up in here."

While Ki was moving Spud, Jessie and Greg finished arranging the scene that would greet the mysterious "boss" when he arrived. Greg was reluctant to handle Beggs's body until he saw Jessie trying to raise the limp, unwieldy corpse, then he swallowed his distaste and helped her to place the dead gunman in a chair, propped up facing the door. Ki came back to join them.

"It looks very convincing," he said. "We should—" He broke off and held up a hand. From outside, the clopping of an approaching horse's hooves was growing steadily louder.

"We'd better get in place," Jessie said.

Ki moved to the front door, Jessie stepped through

45

the broken door of the room where she'd been imprisoned, and Greg went into the room where Ki had taken Spud. The hoofbeats grew closer and stopped.

A heavy footfall sounded on the doorstep, then there came a quick, hard knock on the door. Jessie nodded to Ki. He swung the door open just as Spud's voice rose in a yell of pain and alarm from the room where he and Greg were concealed.

Jessie did not hesitate. She stepped into the opening and brought up the derringer, the handcuffs hampering her movement so that she took longer than usual in bringing the stubby little gun into action. She got a quick glimpse of the man standing in the doorway, a black suit and a derby hat, a hawklike nose in a bearded face.

She aimed as Ki leaped around the open door. The bearded man turned and ran just as Jessie fired. The running man staggered, but did not stop. Ki followed him. A shot sounded from the closed room occupied by Greg and Spud, and a second shot echoed the first. Before its echoes had died away, a shot rang out from outside the house. Then there was silence, broken only by the thudding of the horse's hooves fading in the distance.

★

Chapter 5

Seeing Ki disappear into the darkness, Jessie let him handle the pursuit of the fleeing "boss" and hurried to the closed room to investigate the shooting. She threw the door open. Spud lay across a bed, motionless, his revolver still clutched in his hand. Jessie saw at a glance that the little man was dead. Greg stood in the center of the room, the pistol Ki had given him hanging from his right hand. His left hand was spread across his chest, and blood welled between his fingers.

"I—I guess he shot me," Greg said in a surprised voice when he saw Jessie. "I don't understand it, though. I'm bleeding, but I don't hurt."

Jessie took the gun from Greg's hand, led him into the lighted room, and got him seated in the chair they'd put across the table from Beggs's body.

"Let me take a look," she said, unbuttoning Greg's shirt and pulling its tails from his trousers. Greg was still too shocked by his experience to protest. Even when Jessie slid her strong fingers into the slit the bullet had made in his cotton singlet, and ripped the blood-soaked fabric to allow her to get to the wound, he said nothing.

Jessie looked at the wound. It was superficial, a shallow crease along Greg's ribs, low on the left side of his chest. A trickle of blood ran from the narrow trough the slug had cut.

"It's not bad at all," Jessie assured him. "Nothing but a scratch."

She glanced around, seeking a bandage, and saw the cloth that had been used to gag her, lying where Spud had thrown it on the floor. She picked it up and unrolled it, tore it into wide strips, and took her handkerchief from her jacket pocket. Jessie looked at Greg's wound again, and folded the handkerchief into a flat strip that would cover it. Tying the strips of cloth from the gag together produced a single strip long enough to pass around Greg's chest. She was standing looking at the wound, the strip of cloth in her handcuffed hands, when Ki came in. His nostrils were distended and he was breathing deeply.

"His horse outran me," he announced. "I almost had my hands on him, but he shot at me and I had to drop to the ground and roll. By the time I got back on my feet and began running, he had such a start that I couldn't catch up."

"You're just in time to help me put this bandage on Greg," Jessie said. "That small man they called Spud shot him."

They got the bandage around Greg's chest and knotted the ends. Jessie stepped back and looked at it.

"It's not fancy," she told Greg. "But it'll keep you from bleeding until we can put on a better one."

"Thank you, Jessie. I don't suppose I'm really hurt badly, but it's the first time I've been shot."

"I'm the one who should be doing the thanking," she replied. "It's because of me that all this has happened."

"You think you know who's behind it, then?" Greg asked.

"Perhaps," she hedged. She turned to Ki. "Did you get a good look at the man you were chasing?"

Ki shook his head. "Not even as good a look as you did. He was facing you when I opened the door, but he turned away from me before I got more than a glimpse of him. I did get a good look at his back, though." Ki did not smile when he said this.

Jessie anticipated his next question. "It wasn't anyone we've seen before. That's not surprising, of course."

"I don't understand all this," Greg broke in. "I don't want to act like a lawyer who's cross-examining you, but I do—"

"Please, Greg," Jessie interrupted. "Be patient. There's no time for us to talk right now."

"Jessie's right," Ki agreed. "We need to get back to the hotel, where we won't be as vulnerable as we are in an isolated place like this."

"I suppose I can understand that much," Greg said. "But I still want to know—"

"Later," Jessie broke in. "We'll talk on the way to town." She turned to Ki. "Let's leave the light burning and close the door. You handle the carriage. You know better than either of us how to get back to town."

"I wasn't really looking on my way out, but there's only one road we can take," Ki said. "I think the wise thing to do is for me to let you and Greg off at the hotel. Then I'll drive the carriage to a saloon or to one of the railroad depots and just walk away from it."

"That's as good a plan as any," Jessie nodded. She started to take Greg's arm.

Ki said, "Wait just a minute, Jessie." He stepped over to Beggs's body, still propped in the chair, and bent over it.

"You're surely not going to—" Greg began.

Ki straightened up and showed him the handcuff key.

Greg's mouth formed an O, and he subsided. Ki freed Jessie's wrists and dropped her handcuffs to the floor. Jessie took Greg's arm to help him from the chair, but he pulled away from her and rose to his feet unaided.

"I'm all right," he said. "My side's a little sore, but it's nothing I can't stand."

"We'll ask about a doctor when we get to the hotel," Jessie said as they walked outside to the carriage. She and Greg got in while Ki mounted to the driver's seat. He turned the carriage into the road and they started back toward San Antonio.

"Now will you please tell me what all this is about?" Greg asked as the landau lurched over the dirt road.

Jessie had been deciding how much she should tell the young attorney, and had an answer ready. "You're used to business wars, Greg. The men building railroads aren't exactly angels."

"No. I've seen enough to know that. But aside from that battle the Denver & Rio Grande had with the Santa Fe at Pueblo a year or so ago, there hasn't been any gunfire or bloodshed."

"Father's business enemies are rougher," Jessie replied, her voice growing bitter. "Who do you think murdered him?"

"Why, I heard he was killed in a fight with some cattle thieves, on your Circle Star Ranch."

"Yes, that was the official story," Jessie said. "The men who killed him weren't cattle thieves, though. And I've picked up the fight he was carrying on, you see. There's far too much involved for me to tell you quickly, Greg."

"And that's why you were abducted tonight?"

"I'm sure it is, even if I can't prove it. I haven't any idea how those men knew Ki and I were in San Antonio. For all I know, they may have had someone watching the ranch, who wired ahead that we were on the train.

Will you just take my word that Ki and I were targets, that we didn't come here looking for trouble, or even expecting any?"

"Yes," Greg replied promptly. "I do believe you, Jessie. And if I can help—"

"You helped tonight. But I don't want anyone else involved in my problems, Greg." Jessie leaned over and brushed her lips lightly on his cheek. "Thank you for believing me."

To Jessie and Greg, the ride back to San Antonio's paved but deserted streets seemed much shorter than the trip to the house had been. When they finally reached the business section, half the streetlights had been turned out, but Ki had no trouble finding his way to the hotel.

"I don't think there's anything for us to talk over tonight, is there?" Jessie asked Ki after she and Greg had gotten out of the landau in the porte-cochere of the Menger.

Ki shook his head. "No. They'll have enough to do cleaning up that house," he said with a grim little smile. "We won't be bothered the rest of the night. By the time they finish out there, it'll be daylight."

"I'll see you at breakfast in the restaurant, then."

"That's fine, Jessie. Sleep well."

Ki drove off. Jessie and Greg went into the hotel and stopped at the desk for their room keys. The clerk's eyes lost their sleepiness when he saw Greg's bloodied shirt.

Jessie said quickly, "Mr. Hendricks was injured slightly, by accident. Is there a resident doctor in the hotel?"

"Yes, Miss Starbuck, but he's not here tonight. I can send the night bellman out to find one, if you'd like."

"Perhaps that won't be necessary," she replied. "Do you know where we could find some bandages at this hour?"

"Oh, of course. We keep a roll or two and some

sticking plaster in the kitchen. The cooks are always cutting themselves. If you don't mind waiting a minute?"

"Of course not," she said, then added, "Oh, yes, will you stop at the bar and bring us a bottle of brandy?"

"You really don't need to worry about me, Jessie," Greg protested when the desk clerk disappeared through a door at the back of the lobby. "You said yourself that I only got a scratch. The bandage you put on will be fine until morning."

"No," Jessie replied firmly. "I feel responsible for your being shot. The least I can do is bandage you properly."

"Well . . . if you insist."

Greg's room was on the second floor. He took Jessie's elbow as they mounted the stairs, and held it as they walked down the hall. Inside his room, Jessie slipped off her jacket and pulled up the sleeves of her clinging silk blouse.

"Now take off your coat and shirt, Greg," she said. "Unbutton your underwear too, while you're at it, and slip your arms out of the sleeves. While you do that, I'll step into your bathroom and get some towels and wash my hands."

When Jessie came back into the room, Greg was standing in front of the bureau. He'd obeyed her instructions to strip to the waist; his bloody singlet hung down over his trousers, and his coat and shirt were draped over the back of a chair. He had opened the bottle of brandy and was splashing some of the liquor into a tumbler. He saw Jessie in the mirror and smiled at her.

"It's been a more exciting night than I'd anticipated," he said. "I didn't pour you any, I didn't know whether . . ." His voice trailed off questioningly.

"I do, and I'd like a swallow very much." She watched Greg pick up another glass and begin pouring. "As for the night—well, I'm sorry I let you in for all this, Greg.

If I'd had any idea what was going to happen, we'd have eaten in the hotel."

"Nonsense. Aside from this little scratch on my ribs, which really doesn't hurt the way I thought a bullet wound would, I've enjoyed it in a strange sort of way."

"You might not enjoy the next few minutes so much," Jessie warned him. "I can see that temporary patch I put on has stuck to your wound, and it's going to smart when I soak it off."

Greg brought her the water tumbler with an inch or so of brandy in it. "We can take time to enjoy this much before you begin on me, can't we?"

"Of course." Jessie took the glass and touched it to his. "To your speedy healing, Greg."

They stood in silence for a few moments, sipping the brandy. Jessie studied Greg's bare chest. He was well muscled, his skin clear, with a sparse covering of fine brown curls. Meanwhile, Greg was looking at Jessie, a small frown pulling his brows together.

"You've got a lot of courage, Jessie," he said at last. "Not just when you're in a dangerous situation, the way we were at that house, but now. I don't know many ladies who'd be in a man's hotel room alone, especially after midnight."

"Because they'd be afraid people would talk?" she asked, her lips curling into a smile. "I've learned not to care too much about the things people say. I'm my own woman, Greg. I do as I please and answer to no one but myself."

"Yes, I'm beginning to see that."

Jessie drained the small amount of brandy left in her glass and said, "If you're just making conversation to delay letting me fix that wound, you're not going to get away with it." Her smile took away any sting Greg might have imagined to be in her words. "Now sit down, and let me get started."

She pulled the small straight-backed chair from the writing desk into a clear spot and had Greg sit down straddling it, his hands clutching the back, then she moistened the corner of a towel with some of the brandy. She untied the strip of cloth and looked at the handkerchief, clotted and stiff with blood, that still clung to his wound.

"This will sting a bit after a few minutes," she cautioned him. "But it'll hurt less than ripping that old bandage off."

Jessie began daubing the handkerchief with the towel. Greg sat still, saying nothing, but when the alcohol soaked into the handkerchief and began biting the raw flesh beneath, his hands tightened on the back of the chair. Jessie kept moistening the towel and applying it to the handkerchief. She lifted an edge of the cloth, found it loose, and decided the time had come. With a quick tug she yanked the clotted handkerchief away. Greg unhaled sharply and his muscles tightened again, but he remained silent.

"You can relax now," Jessie told him as she examined the shallow red groove in his side. "The worst is over. I'll make a pad from a length of this bandage and hold it in place with sticking plaster around the edges."

She had him stand up while she folded a length of the bandage and applied it to the raw wound. She began putting plaster around the edges of the cloth, her warm hands traveling over the skin of Greg's side and chest as she smoothed the plaster in place.

"I like feeling your hands on my skin, Jessie," Greg said softly, almost whispering. "I almost wish I had another wound for you to bandage."

"What makes you think I don't enjoy feeling your skin, too?" she asked, looking up into his eyes. She ran her palms around Greg's chest and began stroking his back.

"Be careful, Jessie," he warned smilingly. "I might take that as an invitation."

"Do you really need one?"

Greg put his arms around her and stroked her back softly through the thin, smooth silk of her blouse before he drew her into an embrace. Jessie turned her face up to his, and their lips met in a long and clinging kiss. She offered him her tongue by running it along his closed lips. They opened at her touch and the kiss grew more and more prolonged as their tongues entwined.

"Shall I put out the light?" Greg asked in a half-whisper as they broke off the kiss. "Or do you care?"

"I'm not afraid of the light, Greg."

Jessie's hands were traveling over Greg's back, shoulders, and chest, stroking his skin. She felt his fingers unbuttoning the waistband of her skirt, and twisted her hips to let it slide to the floor. She wore silk knickers under the skirt, tucked into the tops of her boots. Greg looked at the boots and hesitated for a moment, but Jessie levered them off quickly.

When Greg started to slide his hands slid under her blouse, seeking her breasts, Jessie quickly pulled free the knot that held the blouse closed at her throat and shrugged it off her shoulders. Greg's fingers got entangled with the straps of her camisole, and she pulled the camisole down to follow the blouse. He bent his head and began to caress her bared breasts with his mouth and tongue.

Jessie shivered with ecstasy as her nipples hardened under his touch. Her hands went to Greg's belt buckle and then to his fly when the buckle yielded. She pushed the trousers and his cut-off singlet down, and her hand sought Greg's crotch. To her surprise, he was limp, not even beginning to swell. Jessie cradled the lax shaft in her hands, stroking it gently. She felt it swell slightly in response to her caressing, but it did not stiffen to an erection.

"What's wrong, Greg?" she whispered. "Don't I please you?"

"Oh, God, it's not that, Jessie! I want you more than any woman I've ever seen. And this never has happened to me before. Be patient, please. Give me time."

"Let's lie down," she suggested. "We're not in any hurry. You're tense and tired. Maybe relaxing on the bed will help."

Greg slid his shoes off and stepped away from his trousers. Jessie led him to the bed and lay down beside him. She held his flaccid shaft lightly in one hand while she caressed his chest and neck and shoulders with her lips and tongue. Although she was aroused and ready herself, Jessie had learned that there were times when men needed an extra stimulus to make their bodies respond.

Slowly, Jessie carried her caresses down Greg's muscular body until her cheek rubbed against his lax member. She caressed it with butterfly kisses, then encircled it with her lips and began to work her tongue over and around the tip. She felt Greg's body grow taut and then relax as she continued her caresses, and slowly the shaft in her mouth began to swell. Greg moaned as he grew stiffer, and Jessie was careful not to carry her caresses too far. Besides, she was more than ready now, and needed him in a more conventional manner.

When she was sure the time had come, Jessie released Greg and knelt above him, her thighs straddling his hips. She positioned his quivering sex and sank down on it slowly, reveling in the feeling of his hard manhood penetrating her, filling her.

She rotated her hips slowly, then faster, surprised at the speed with which her sensations were mounting. Her frenzy grew swiftly. Her hips rose and fell, and she did not slow her frantic gyrations or try to control the rush of her climax, but let herself go, her body jerking in a drawn-out ecstasy as she mounted to the peak and fell forward on Greg, gasping and shaking and satisfied.

For several minutes she lay still, while the waves of her climax settled and passed. Greg still filled her, firmly erect. He began to stroke her soft buttocks, and then his hand crept down to feel their joining. He traced the juncture with his fingertip. Jessie quivered as she felt the finger slipping along her moist, taut flesh, and she stirred.

"Is it too soon to start over, Jessie?" Greg asked her. "I think I'm myself again."

"Start, then," she replied. "I'm as ready as you are."

Greg rolled above her and Jessie slid her thighs up to his hips, clasping her legs tightly over his back. He rose and almost withdrew, then thrust into her with a swfit lunge that sent him deeper than Jessie had been able to take him while she was on top. She sighed happily as she felt him driving into her with stroke after stroke, and once more her body began quivering as she approached climax.

"Oh, now, Greg, now!" Jessie cried, spreading her thighs wide to let him go deeper.

Greg responded with a flurry of faster, harder strokes, and Jessie was soon lost in her feelings. Her pelvis slammed against his as Greg kept up the drumbeat tempo of his lunges. Her sensations overwhelmed her and her hips rose to meet him in a quick tattoo of frenzied motion while body overpowered brain and she reached her climax with a smothered shriek. She was dimly aware that Greg had stopped moving and was lying on her, warm and heavy. Jessie lay with her eyes closed, satiated for the moment, while the frenzy faded.

They lay still, remaining entwined for what seemed

like a long time, whispering to each other, murmuring softly. Gradually the stress of the preceding hours overtook them. At some point, Greg rolled off Jessie's exhausted, satisfied body, and they were both asleep in seconds.

★

Chapter 6

Jessie and Ki reined in and looked across the rippling ocher surface of the Prairie Dog Town Fork of the Red River. The sun was slanting low, its reddening beams in their eyes, for their second day on the trail was drawing to a close. After leaving the little cluster of houses that had grown like mushrooms around the railroad station at Wichita Falls, they'd ridden steadily west, keeping to the riverbank.

During the two-day ride they'd passed fewer than a dozen houses, most of them set well away from the stream. Now, on the opposite bank, cutting though the gently rolling hills, they saw the shallow valley they'd been looking for. The Sweetwater Fork flowed through it to join the Prairie Dog Town Fork and combine the many-forked stream into a single river.

"I don't like it," Ki said. "We're in quicksand country."

Jessie replied, "It doesn't look too deep, Ki. And the current's gentle."

"There's no trail here to show it's a crossing," Ki pointed out. "Even if this river's like so many others, a mile wide and a half-inch deep, the bottom could be treacherous."

"If we cross here, I'll go first," Jessie offered. "Sun

can feel quicksand under his hooves and pull back faster than any horse I've ever ridden."

Ki shook his head.

"There's an hour or more of daylight left. Let's ride on upstream and see if there aren't signs of a crossing ahead."

Jessie nodded, and they nudged the horses ahead. A half-mile farther on, they found what Ki had suggested they might, a well-marked trail that led into the wide stream, its continuation clearly visible on the opposite bank. They splashed across the ford, seldom more than fetlock-deep. On the north bank, a hundred yards from the river, the trail dipped into a shallow dale.

A gentle, sparsely grassed slope, dotted thickly with low-growing mesquite, rose from three sides of the hollow. Many of the head-high bushes were dead or dying, and the black circles of dead fires in the glade were evidence that many others had stopped in the sheltered spot before them. Jessie reined in.

"This looks like as good a place as any to stop," she suggested. "Even if we push on, we won't get much farther before dark."

Jessie swung out of the saddle and stretched. After changing in Wichita Falls to her trail outfit of shirt and tight denim jeans, she felt really comfortable for the first time since they'd left the Circle Star.

They made camp quickly, in the manner of experienced travelers. Ki took the panniers off the packhorse and unsaddled all three animals before leading them to a grassy spot to stake them out for the night. Jessie gathered an armful of dead mesquite limbs and kindled a small fire before spreading their bedrolls.

By the time Ki returned after watering and staking out the horses, Jessie had bacon and potatoes sizzling and the coffeepot bubbling. They sat cross-legged on the ground to eat, and after the meal, while they drank a final cup of coffee, Jessie looked out into the darkness and turned to Ki.

"Do you think we need to stand watch tonight?" she asked.

"No. I've kept an eye on our backtrail ever since we left the railroad. If anybody is following us, they're better at trailing than I am at watching."

"It's not like the cartel to give up so easily, Ki."

"We both know they haven't given up. But I think they were so sure of taking us in San Antonio that they didn't plan beyond that. And we gave them an unpleasant surprise there."

"Our trail wouldn't be hard to pick up, of course," Jessie went on thoughtfully. "We haven't made any effort to cover it."

"Trying to cover our trail in country like this would be a waste of time, Jessie," Ki pointed out. "Even a cold trail's easy to follow when there's no way to get lost in a crowd."

"That works two ways, Ki," she said. "If we stand out like sore thumbs, so would anybody following us. So we won't start worrying until they catch up with us. One thing we can be sure of. They will, sooner or later."

Sundown of the next day found Jessie and Ki making a dry camp on the flat, endless prairie that lay in the vee between the two forks of the Red River. They'd left the Sweetwater Fork before noon, at the end of the rough horseshoe bend into which the stream swept and curved far to the east. Another half-day to the north, they'd pick up the river once more where the bend began, and follow it until they reached the landmarks given them in Dave Clemson's letter.

At sunrise they were on the move again, still riding across the rich grassland they had entered soon after crossing the Prairie Dog Town Fork. From horizon to horizon the land swept in rippling waves, broken only by an occasional rounded bluff or by the jagged scar of a narrow red-rock canyon. The grass was knee-high to their horses' legs and was just beginning its transition from summer green to the straw-yellow hue of winter.

Jessie looked around and said to Ki, "If all of Greer County's like this, it's easy to see why Dave wants as much land here as he can get. This is prime cattle range."

"Yes, and if Dave is reaching for more than his share, you can be sure there are others doing the same thing," Ki replied. "From what I've heard about the rest of the Indian Territory, there's no place else that's as good as this for raising cattle."

They rode on through the long morning, and reached the banks of the Sweetwater Fork again in early afternoon, at the point where the horseshoe bend started. There was no beaten trail along the bank here, as there had been to the south, and only occasionally did Jessie and Ki see any signs of other travelers as they followed the course of the stream. In late afternoon, on the northern horizon, a line of low, jagged bluffs became visible, with higher, smoother humps beyond, both obscured by the heat haze that turned the air into a shimmering veil.

Jessie pointed. "There's Dave's landmark, the Quartz Mountains, he called them."

"I wouldn't exactly call them mountains," Ki said. "But they're the first and only high country we've seen, and they're about where they ought to be, according to his letter. It's time for us to turn west, then."

They set their course by the sun now, and rode due west. As Clemson had written in his directions, after a two-hour ride they reached a stream, more creek than river, narrow and shallow. The river flowed south and they rode upstream, turning west again as the watercourse made a bend. After they'd spent another hour in the saddle, the angular lines of buildings grew visible ahead.

"That must be Dave's place," Jessie told Ki. "He said the C-Dot is the only ranch for twenty miles around."

With their goal in sight now, they sped up, urging the trail-tired horses to a faster walk. Soon they could make out details of the ranch: a rambling, low house of boards that were still yellow-fresh, a narrow bunkhouse to one side, the barn and corral and hay sheds visible beyond the house.

"It's Dave's ranch, all right," Ki said. "He wrote that he was still trying to get it finished, and those buildings are so new that they haven't had time to weather."

Jessie and Ki were still more than a mile from the ranch house when a rider appeared, swerving around the house from the direction of the corral. He cut in front of the house and started north, his horse gaining speed, then suddenly reined in, turned his mount, and headed for Jessie and Ki.

"That's Dave!" Jessie exclaimed as the rider came closer. "I've seen him riding up to the Circle Star main house too many times to mistake him." She stood up in her stirrups and waved, and the oncoming man returned the greeting.

Ki said, "I got the idea he was starting to go somewhere else when he saw us."

Jessie nodded and touched Sun's flank with her toe. The big palomino moved forward. Ki matched her faster pace, and within a few moments the three riders met and reined in.

"Dave!" Jessie said. "It's good to see you again!"

"You're sort of a sight for sore eyes too, Jessie," Clemson said. "And you too, Ki. You look chipper, like always."

"So do you, Dave," Ki replied. "I think you've even put on a pound or two since you left the Circle Star."

"Well, since I got married and get good home cooking again, it ain't surprising," Clemson smiled. "Come on.

63

Let's get on to the house. I want you to get acquainted with Nettie."

In spite of Ki's comment about his weight gain, Dave Clemson was a spare man, his shoulders wide but without depth or bulk. His chest tapered sharply to his waist, the knobs of his knees showing in sharp outline under his jeans. His face had the saddle-leather hue and texture of those men who, in any kind of weather, spent their days on the open range. His eyes were deep set under grizzled brows, and his nose was a fractured triangle. He wore a full, untrimmed mustache, grizzled like his brows, that trailed down in a swooping curve below the ends of his lips.

"Don't let us break into your work, Dave," Jessie said as they rode abreast toward the house. "You started north as though you had some good reason for being in a hurry."

Clemson hesitated for a moment, then said soberly, "Things are a mite upset, Jessie. I don't guess I said anything in my last letter about Retha, but if you'll recall, I mentioned her when I wrote to tell you I was marrying Nettie."

"Of course, Retha's your stepdaughter. What about her, Dave?" Jessie asked.

"Well, this is slack time on the place." Dave talked with slow deliberation. "Soon as we got the market herd drove down to railhead, I paid off all my hands but one and let 'em go. Fred—he's the one I kept on—he's been riding herd by hisself. A week or so back, he had to move the herd I'm wintering, and I went up to help. I stayed a day or so longer'n I meant to, so Nettie got nervous and sent Retha up yesterday to see was I all right. But I got back last night, and I didn't meet her on the way, and when she didn't come in today, Nettie got spooked. So I was starting out to backtrack when I seen you."

"Hadn't you better go on, then?" Jessie suggested. "You don't have to ride with us right to your door. I imagine your wife's looking for us."

"Well, not exactly, Jessie. I wasn't sure when you'd get here, or even if you'd come at all."

"That shouldn't make any difference, though. She'd know who we are from hearing you talk about us. And if you're anxious to find your stepdaughter, I'd hate to delay you."

"Oh, I ain't worried about Retha, even if Nettie is. The fool girl likely piddled a lot of time away riding up, and didn't feel like coming back in the dark last night." Clemson paused and frowned, then added, "Acourse, that don't explain why she ain't showed up yet."

"But if your wife's worried, maybe you'd better go ahead and check up on Retha," Ki said. "I'll be glad to ride with you."

"Why, I wouldn't ask you to do that," Dave replied. "You two been riding all the way from the railroad, and I know what a haul that is."

"It's an easy ride," Jessie told him. "I'm not tired, and I'm sure Ki isn't, either."

"For an honest fact, Jessie, I don't see much use of going," Dave shrugged. "This ain't the first time Retha's gone kiting off someplace and not come back when she said she would. I appreciate your offering, Ki, but I'll head out early tomorrow for a look-see if she don't get back tonight."

On the veranda that stretched across the main C-Dot house, a chubby woman was waiting when they rode up. She had a comfortably rounded face and a figure that was a bit more than voluptuous, and wore her dark hair piled high in a bun at the top of her head. She appeared to be a dozen years younger than Dave.

The rancher swung off his horse and walked up to the veranda, and Jessie and Ki followed.

"Nettie, say hello to Miss Jessie Starbuck and Ki," Dave said. "You heard me talk about 'em enough to know who they are. I told you I figured my letter'd bring 'em here for a visit, and sure enough, it did."

"Miss Starbuck, I'm right glad I'm finally getting to meet you," Nettie said. "And Mr. Ki, too. Like Dave said, I sure enough do know who you folks are."

"We're glad to meet you," Jessie replied. "And we're not 'miss' and 'mister,' we're Jessie and Ki to Dave, and to you too."

"That's just real sweet of you, Jessie. Come on in now. I guess Dave'll see to your horses before he starts out again to look for Retha."

"I keep telling you, Retha's all right," Clemson said. "My guess is she missed me and Fred because we'd left the old camp, and she followed the winter herd's trail up to that north range. She might've swung by the village up at the Quartzes before she come home. You know she's got a girl chum or two up there."

"That may be so," Nettie said, her worried frown relaxing. "But I worry just the same."

"Well, give over worrying while I get Jessie and Ki settled in. You folks go inside with Nettie. I'll see to your horses," Dave told his friends.

"I'll go along with you, Dave," Ki volunteered. "Jessie, I'll bring our gear in. You go on with Mrs. Clemson."

Jessie followed Nettie into the ranch house. The main room was a long rectangle, sparsely furnished, with a dining table at one end, near a door that Jessie assumed led to the kitchen. Through archways at each end of the room she could see halls leading to bedrooms on each side of the house.

"I'm sorry we're sorta tore up," Nettie said, gesturing Jessie to an easy chair and settling herself on the sofa. "But I guess Dave's told you, he's been gone a week or more and now my little girl ain't come home when she oughta. But we'll make you as comfortable as we can while you're here."

"Please don't go to any trouble," Jessie said. "Just treat us like family, that's how we think of Dave."

"Don't you worry about being trouble," Nettie replied. "My hired girl stayed on to clean up after the roundup hands left, and I'll keep her awhile yet. Now I do hope you ain't too starved, because it'll be a little while before supper's on the table. Sunny's been busy cleaning up the bunkhouse all day. Them roundup hands Dave hired left it in a awful mess."

"Sunny?" Jessie asked.

"Oh, that's my 'Rapaho girl help. Her Indian name's Bright Sunrise, but that's too big a mouthful. She works good most of the time, 'cept when she goes kiting off, like Retha's done."

"I'm sure your daughter's all right," Jessie said. "She probably went by the village Dave spoke of to visit her friends. It probably didn't occur to her that you'd be worried."

"Well, I'd worry a sight more about her being at that little shack town than I would if she was sleeping on the prairie. You know, they say there's outlaw hideouts in them Quartzes, and that settlement's where they go to do their trading. Why, I've even heard about one place in the Quartzes they call Outlaw Mountain."

Before Jessie could reply, Dave came in, followed by Ki, who carried their saddlebags in one hand, their rifles in the other.

"Now, Nettie, let's don't be passing gossip," Dave told his wife. He had obviously overheard her last remark as he led Ki in through the kitchen, for he went on, "All we know about outlaws hiding in the Quartzes is just talk. I ain't covered the place good, because I've been too busy, but I sure don't put much stock in that outlaw stuff."

"That's well and good for you to say," Nettie sniffed. She went on, "It's going to be too dark for you to see Retha, if you don't get started right away."

"I wish you'd quit fretting," Dave told her. "Retha's big enough now so she don't need to hang on your apron strings no more."

"If she don't get home tomorrow, do you promise solemn that you'll go out and find her, Dave?" Nettie asked.

"You know I will. I'd of gone now, except for Jessie and Ki getting here." He turned to them and said, "And don't you feel bad about me putting it off, because I know Retha's all right. Now you go on and settle in. We'll have supper on the table pretty soon, and afterwards we can set and talk."

When supper was over, the four settled down in the main room. Jessie and Ki answered Dave's questions about the Circle Star, and she was relieved when her ex-foreman avoided any mention of the days before Alex's death. As Dave's reminiscing began to wear thin, Jessie adroitly guided their talk to his experiences since he'd left the Starbuck range.

"Well, over in the Panhandle, I stumbled over some farmers from back East who'd gone in together to buy one of them old Mexican land grants," Clemson told them. "They was about busted from trying to raise crops on land that was good cattle range, but not much else. I struck a good enough bargain; they didn't want much except enough money to go back East on."

"But it was big enough to run a good herd on?" Jessie asked.

"Big enough for anyplace else. I had to do some Texas-style claiming, but I'd learned the ropes by then. So I wound up with a pretty good spread. Not big like the *real* big ones—Goodnight's or Cresswell's or Bugbee's and all like them, and it wouldn't stack up as such a much alongside the Circle Star—but good enough for me. Then I lucked out."

"That would have been the Englishman you mentioned in your letters," Jessie said.

"Oh, I can't complain, Jessie," Dave told her. "I never did see folks go panting after cattle range like they did. There wasn't much place to go but the Panhandle by then, and most of them foreigners had more money than brains. So, when one of them syndicates come along and bought the spreads on three sides of me, I knew all I had to do was bide my time."

"And the syndicate offered to buy you out so they could make their spread complete," Ki guessed.

"That's just what happened," Dave grinned. "I set back and waited till they upped the bid three times, then I said yes. I'd heard about Greer County, you see. When the fuss busted out over whether it belonged to Texas or the United States, I figured if a man had a good enough title, whoever won the argument was either going to have to say his title was good, or buy him out."

"From the way you talk, Dave, you don't care whether you keep your spread here or not," Jessie frowned.

"To lay it right on the line, Jessie, I don't. If I get my title clear, I'll stay on and work the place, a'course."

"Is that what you'd rather do?" she asked.

"Well, I've worked pretty hard all my life, Jessie," Dave answered thoughtfully. "But there's going to come a day when I'll feel like quitting, and whichever way the deal goes, I'll have enough money so me and Nettie can live high on the hog anyplace we want to, for as long as we're alive. I don't see how I can lose, whichever way it goes."

"But in your letter—" Jessie began.

Dave interrupted her. "I better tell you about why I wrote that letter, Jessie. You know how I felt about Alex, and how I feel about you."

She nodded. "Yes, I suppose I do. You were my teacher on the Circle Star for a long time, almost like a second father when Dad was away."

"I ain't forgot it, either. And I know how Alex come to be murdered by them damn foreigners in what you and him call the cartel. And Alex done more for me than anybody else ever did, seeing as I didn't ever know my own daddy and mother."

Clemson stopped and swallowed hard. The others sat silent, waiting for him to continue. The silence was becoming oppressive when Jessie broke it.

"Go on, Dave," she said quietly. "We're listening."

"Well, I didn't want to put nothing on paper," Dave said. "But there's been funny things happening here in Greer County of late. And I don't want nobody that's against you to do you harm, Jessie. But I'll tell you the truth, I'm getting spooked."

"What are you trying to tell me, Dave?" Jessie asked.

"I'm trying to say that I got more than a little bit of a hunch that them men in the cartel, the ones that's give you Starbucks so much grief, are trying to take over Greer County."

★

Chapter 7

For a moment, Jessie was too surprised to speak. Ki, too, sat silent after hearing Dave Clemson announce his suspicions.

Jessie finally asked, "What makes you think the cartel would want a place like Greer County, Dave?"

"You know I never had much real schooling, Jessie, but just by watching them foreign crooks fight Alex and then you, and seeing how you fought 'em back, I learned things schools don't teach a man. I figure them cartel people are after a lot more'n just Starbuck property. Looks to me like that ain't but a start to 'em taking over the whole country, then maybe even the world."

When Dave paused for breath, Jessie said, "That was Alex's idea too, Dave. His fight against the cartel wasn't just to protect Starbuck property, but to keep its bosses from getting more of a foothold in the United States."

"I'd take your father's judgment on a thing like that anytime, Jessie. Now if that outfit's aiming so high, they'd need a lot of men, wouldn't they? And a big place where they could have a sorta headquarters?"

Ki said quickly, "Of course they would, Dave. They have a good start now, but they'd need a whole lot more."

"And the way I see it, they'd need a place where the

law couldn't touch 'em, a place where they'd *be* the law. Like here."

"Greer County," Jessie nodded. "Yes. It would make a perfect central headquarters."

"Right here where we're sitting is about as near to being the bellybutton of the United States as you can get," Dave said.

Ki added, "It's not only in the middle of the country, it doesn't have many people in it, no cities or towns. And the way the railroads are building, it's going to be easy to get from here to just about anywhere in the country in another few years."

"It's likely to take a long time for Texas and Washington to get their fuss settled over which one it belongs to," Dave pointed out. "By then, that cartel outfit could just about be set up as another state, and they'd be the government of it."

"It's a frightening idea," Jessie said. "I wouldn't want to see it happen." Frowning thoughtfully, she looked at Clemson and asked, "What gave you the idea something like that could be going on, Dave?"

"A lot of things that's took place just lately, Jessie. Like Nettie was saying to you right after you got here, there's been a lot more talk about Outlaw Mountain—"

Nettie broke in, "But you keep saying that's just gossip, Dave. You told me I ought not be talking about that place."

"So I did, Nettie," he agreed. "If them cartel people is moving in here, they'd be likely to shut off that kind of gossip by putting a bullet into whoever's spreading it."

"What else made you suspicious, Dave?" Jessie asked.

"Somebody's been trying to get hold of the land north of my spread, Jessie. That'd take in them Quartz Mountains and a lot of other broke-up land. Thing is, none of that country's good for ranching or farming or anything else. Nobody is his right mind would give a plugged nickel for it."

"There must be something else, though," Ki said.

"What else there is, Ki, is just an idea that popped into my head a little bit ago. I don't know if it'd make sense to anybody else, but it does to me."

"What's your idea, Dave?" Jessie asked.

"Well, if them cartel folks is looking for a lot of men, they'd find a bunch of the meanest fighters in the country right at their back door, in the Indian Nation."

"They certainly would," Jessie frowned.

"Them wild tribes, the Comanche and Sioux and Cheyenne and Kiowa, they sure don't have much use for the federal government, or for Texas either," Dave went on. "It took more'n ten years and about ten soldiers for every Indian to get 'em tucked away on them reservations over in the Nation. And the Indians didn't have much to fight with, either. How'd it be if somebody was to give 'em good rifles and cannon and suchlike?"

"But there are soldiers on duty over in the Nation, Dave," Ki protested. "They'd stop any sort of uprising."

"There ain't as many soldiers in the Nation as you'd think, Ki. How many would you guess?"

Ki thought for a moment and shook his head. "I suppose I don't really have any idea. I just imagined there'd be a lot."

"Well, there ain't. All that's left is two or three artillery batteries at Fort Sill, that's about sixty miles east of here, on Cache Crick. A hundred miles to the northeast, on the Canadian, I'd say two hundred soldiers is at Fort Reno. Then, way north about a hundred and fifty miles, there's Fort Supply, but that's just a quartermaster depot, and there'd only be maybe fifty regulars there."

"And that's all?" Jessie asked when Dave fell silent.

"Unless you want to count Fort Gibson, way to the east, just this side of the Arkansas line," Dave said. "And it's a quartermaster depot, like Fort Supply."

"You've been thinking about this for quite a while, haven't you, Dave?" Jessie asked.

"I been studying it considerable, Jessie," Dave said. "Especially of late. That's why I wrote you the way I did, not coming right out with anything that somebody else might catch on to if they was to read that letter, but hinting around in a way I was pretty sure you'd understand."

"But what do you think Ki and I can do, Dave?"

"I don't rightly know. I guess I figured you'd know somebody back East in Washington, somebody that'd listen to you on account of you're Alex Starbuck's girl. There sure ain't nobody who'd pay much heed to what I say."

Jessie thought about this for a moment, then shook her head. "If I took your story and your ideas to anybody in Washington, they'd think I was crazy, Starbuck or no Starbuck. It's just too unthinkable, Dave."

"But you believe it, don't you?" Clemson asked anxiously.

Again, Jessie sat silently for a moment before she replied, "Yes, I do. It doesn't seem possible, and it would sound—well, as I just said, even crazy, to somebody in the East. But I believe you, Dave."

"So do I," Ki said quietly. "And you're right about trying to get anybody in Washington to take it seriously, Jessie."

"I wouldn't even think of trying to convince anyone in Washington, Ki," Jessie said. "Father used to say the people there don't live in the same world we do. Even those who come from the West change after they've been there a while."

"You mean there's not anything you can do about it?"

Dave asked Jessie, his weatherbeaten face drawn into a worried frown.

"I didn't say that," she answered. "It'd be wasting time to look to the government for help, but that doesn't mean we can't do something ourselves."

Dave stared at her incredulously. "You mean just the three of us?"

"Ki and I have been fighting the cartel by ourselves for a long time now," Jessie replied. "We've beaten them enough times to know it can be done. What we've got to figure out now is how to go about it."

"Outlaw Mountain," Ki said thoughtfully. "If Dave's right, that has to be our starting point."

"Of course," Jessie agreed. "And we won't know how to start until we know what it's like there." She stood up. "We won't get any answers sitting here tonight. Ki, we'd better get some sleep. We'll be riding with Dave when he goes to look for Retha tomorrow."

Ki usually had no trouble sleeping, in spite of the long days he and Jessie spent in the saddle. Though the night was pleasantly cool, Ki's room seemed warm. He was tossing on the bed, waiting for sleep to come, when he heard Sun neighing angrily. He was on his feet in an instant. Slipping on his trousers and vest, he went silently through the dark house and out the back door. There was a quarter moon, and after the almost total darkness of the house, Ki could see clearly in the moonlight. Using the bulk of one of the hay sheds to cover his movement, he started for the corral.

Sun neighed again as Ki reached the shed. He knew the big palomino's ways well enough to recognize that the tone of Sun's neighing indicated neither anger nor alarm, but irritation at having his night's rest disturbed. Ki stopped behind a corner of the hay shed and looked toward the corral. He saw Sun's imposing bulk backed into a far corner of the enclosure. In front of the palomino was a shadowy figure, inching cautiously toward the horse.

Moving silently on slippered feet, Ki half-walked, half-ran to the corral fence. He vaulted the fence, landing almost noiselessly on the other side. Three long strides took him to the shadowy figure standing in front of the horse. Ki grabbed the intruder, using a simple wristlock.

With his quarry's right arm immobilized, Ki completed his capture by wrapping his left hand around and over the captive's mouth. It was not until he tightened his arm around his quarry's chest that Ki realized he was holding a woman.

Ki decided not to release her at once. He hissed into her ear, "I will free your mouth to let you talk, but if you cry out or scream, you will be very sorry. Do you understand me?" With some difficulty, the woman nodded. Ki went on, "Very well, Now tell me who you are and what you're doing here."

"Please," she said. "You have made a big mistake, Mr. Ki. I am Bright Sunrise. I work cleaning house for Mrs. Clemson. I was watching when you and the lady rode up with Mr. Clemson."

Ki relaxed his hold on the girl, but did not release her completely. He asked, "If you work in the house, what are you doing in the corral at this time of night?"

"I sleep in the bunkhouse. But when you and the lady came this afternoon, I saw the fine horse. I wanted to look at him close. Now is the first time I can do this."

Ki could understand the fascination Sun would hold for an Indian. He remembered Nettie's mentioning that Bright Sunrise was an Arapaho, one of the horse tribes. He released the girl. She turned around to face him, and he saw that she was young, perhaps in her early twenties. Her Indian blood showed in her tawny skin and prominent nose, and in her short stature. Ki thought, though, that if he'd met her on a city street, he might not have realized she was an Indian.

"What is your tribe?" she asked. "You do not look like Sioux or Comanche or Cheyenne. You are pale, like a Cherokee, but your nose does not belong to them, or to the Creeks. Are you a River Tribe man? Or of people far to the west?"

Ki smiled. He could tell from her questions that Bright Sunrise must have watched him very closely indeed, at times when he was too preoccupied to notice her.

"My people live across the ocean," he said.

"Ah," Bright Sunrise nodded. "I know about the ocean."

"You speak very good English," Ki observed.

"I have gone to the Jesuit school. Now I am back with my people. Our reservation is just beyond the mountains, across the river. Tell me of this horse, Ki. I have not seen one like it before, so golden and with such a long mane."

"Sun is a palomino. I don't suppose there are many in this part of the country. Why are you so interested?"

"A horse like this would be powerful medicine among my people. My father would trade all the horses of the small herd he has left to get one like Sun."

"Well, Bright Sunrise, as long as I know you're not a horse thief, I'm not going to bother you," Ki said. "You look at Sun all you want to tonight, or tomorrow, in the daylight. I'm going back to bed."

"You will not tell Mrs. Clemson about this, please, Mr. Ki? She does not like for me to talk to the men who are at the ranch."

"I won't say a word," Ki promised. "And my name is just Ki, not Mr. Ki. Good night, Bright Sunrise."

"Good night, Ki."

After he'd vaulted the corral fence, Ki turned once to look at the Arapaho girl before he started for the house.

Bright Sunrise had gone up to Sun and was stroking the palomino's velvety muzzle. Ki shrugged and went back to bed.

By noon the next day, Jessie, Ki, and Dave Clemson were riding east across the trackless prairie. They'd gone to the line camp, but had left at once after finding out from Fred, the cowhand watching the C-Dot herd, that Retha had not been there. Now, with the sun just beginning to slant down from its zenith, Dave had just pointed out a long coulee running roughly parallel to their route, and identified it as the northern boundary of his ranch.

There were no other landmarks that Jessie or Ki could see, except the Quartz Mountains. They loomed against the pale, bright late-summer sky ahead, not as rugged and towering and impressive as a major range such as the Rockies, but an isolated upthrust too high to be shrugged off as hills, looking indeed like mountains as they rose above their flat, featureless surroundings. The tallest and largest peak of the little clump, rising perhaps a thousand feet above the prairie, dominated its fellows. Dave pointed to it.

"That's the one folks hereabouts call Outlaw Mountain," he said. "Not that it's such a much, but it's the highest place in maybe a hundred miles, till you get over east to the Washitas."

"You must have heard something about the mountains, Dave, even if you haven't had time to explore them," Jessie suggested.

"Oh, sure. There's yarns told about caves in 'em, and box canyons, places where the Indians hid their loot back in the wagon train days. Trouble is, nobody seems to know much more'n I do about them hills. I ain't talked to a single soul that admits they ever been up in 'em and looked around."

"We'll soon know whether that's true or not," Ki said.

"If people have explored them, or outlaws have really been using those hills as a hideout, they'll have left tracks somewhere."

They rode on steadily, talking little, making steady progress toward their destination. The country grew more broken as they drew closer to the hills. A few steep-walled but shallow canyons opened in front of them, and it was easier to zigzag around them than to tire the horses by riding down their walls and scrambling up on the far side. The land tilted upward now, as they got closer to the base of the peaks.

"We'll be swinging over to the canyon that leads into them hills pretty soon," Dave told them. "But I'm taking us a couple of miles outta the way because I got a hunch Retha's at that little settlement. Like I told Nettie last night, she's got friends there that she visits once in a while."

"It's none of my business, Dave, but you don't seem to be very much concerned about your stepdaughter," Jessie suggested.

"Oh, I'm concerned for Nettie's sake, but Retha's a right stubborn girl. Her and me never did hit it off too good. She was plumb crazy about her own daddy, and she didn't much like it when me and Nettie got hitched. Nettie told me plain out that I was to go my way and let Retha go hers, so that's what I done."

"As long as it was Nettie's idea, I can't blame you, Dave," Jessie said after a moment's thought. "And judging from what I've heard both of you say, Retha's not too inclined to listen to advice or take suggestions from either of you."

"She ain't," Dave nodded. "But all the same, she's a young girl, and I feel like I'm sorta responsible, just the same as if she was my own."

They rode on, their shadows lengthening ahead of them now, Jessie and Ki following Dave now as he led them across the humped and arroyo-cut terrain that grew more and more rugged as they drew closer to the mountains. At last Dave turned his horse into a valley between two of the low foothills that extended in clusters at the base of the Quartzes. They picked up a trail of sorts at the mouth of the valley, and rode in cool shadows. Dave reined his horse off the trail after they'd wound through the valley for a bit more than two miles, and led the way up one of the hills.

Turning in the saddle, he told Jessie and Ki, "Them folks in the settlement don't cotton much to strangers. If I was by myself, I'd ride on in. They know me there by now. But I'd as soon not take you in, so we'll go up that little hump ahead, where we can look down and watch for a bit without them seeing us."

With rising ground under their hooves, the horses moved more slowly. As they neared the top of the hump, Dave reined in, and Jessie and Ki followed suit. On foot, they followed him around the shoulder of the hill until they could look down on a straggle of thirty or so small shacks, many of them little more than huts, which stood on a wide shelf at the edge of a steep-walled canyon. The houses, for the most part, huddled back from the canyon edge and nestled against the sharply rising shoulder of the hill.

Most of the shacks were of random-width boards, and all but a few of them were weatherbeaten, their walls and roofs patched with pieces of board or flattened tin. Most had pens made of slats or chickenwire at one side, where a few hens and a rooster walked and pecked. There were goats tethered close to a few, a cow at two of them.

A half-dozen people were visible walking around between the huts, men and women, and though the angle from which the three looked down made faces difficult to observe, Jessie could see that many of them were old, and at least half the men carried a shoulder or an arm askew or walked with a limp.

"We'll just stay here and watch a few minutes," Dave said. "It's the slack of the day, time when folks stir around, getting ready to settle in for the night. There's not but one spring, and them folks in the settlement mostly go to it and fill their buckets before they start cooking supper."

Sitting on their heels on the slope above the settlement, the trio watched it slowly stirring to life. Near the center of the settlement, one building larger and better-built than the others seemed to draw most of those who came from the huts.

"That's the store," Dave explained. "It don't carry much goods in stock, but the folks who live there can get flour and cornmeal and sugar and coffee from it."

"As you said, Dave, it's not much of a town," Jessie commented. "I don't see what keeps it alive."

"Well, it's about the only place between the Sweetwater Fork and the Prairie Dog Town Fork where anybody can buy any kind of grub. And the store's got tobacco and keg whiskey, so it gets a little trade from the reservation Indians on the other side of the Quartzes, too. They'll travel quite a ways for a drink, because about all you can buy in the Nation is just raw alcohol with a little molasses and red pepper flavoring." He stopped suddenly and pointed. "I knew I was right! Look, there's Retha."

He pointed, and Jessie and Ki followed his gesture with their eyes. Two young women had appeared among the houses and were walking toward the store. They were about the same age: in their early twenties, as closely as Jessie could tell. Both wore long gingham dresses with full skirts, and were neater in dress and appearance than a majority of the older women.

"She's the one on the right," Dave said.

Retha was a dark blonde who wore her hair loose down her back. Jessie could see her face only when she turned to talk to her companion, who was doing most of the talking. Retha had fair skin and regular features, and at a distance she seemed of a pattern with most of the younger women Jessie had seen on the frontier.

"Well, I'm glad your hunch was right, Dave," Jessie said. "At least you don't have to worry about her now."

"No, but I'd sure like to tan her bottom for getting Nettie so upset by—"

From behind them, a harsh voice broke into Dave's words. "You three stay real still now. I got a gun on you, and any one of you that moves ain't going to see the sun set tonight!"

★

Chapter 8

Jessie and Ki froze and remained silent. Dave froze, but said without turning his head, "I know your voice, mister, and I'll hang a face on it in a minute. And if you been watching us, you'll know all we come up here for was to take a look at the settlement."

"If you wanted to look at it, why didn't you ride on into it, instead of skulking around the way you been doing?" the unseen man asked suspiciously.

Dave did not give a direct reply; instead he said calmly, "I got you placed now. Skip Toland, ain't it?"

For a moment the man said nothing, then he told them grudgingly, "All right. I guess you're telling the truth, Clemson. You people can turn around, but don't make a move beyond that. I still want some answers."

Moving carefully, Jessie, Ki, and Dave turned to face the man who'd challenged them. Jessie examined him with quick flicks of her eyes that did not give away her close scrutiny as a direct stare would have done.

Toland was tall and rawboned, deep in the chest. He was clean-shaven, his cheeks and elongated chin free of stubble. His eyes were as opaque as obsidian chips, his nose thick and heavy—a Comanche nose, Jessie thought. Though the separate garments he had on were like those of any cowhand who might be encountered anywhere on the Texas range, the manner in which he wore them made it very obvious to her that this man was no cowhand.

Toland's shirt collar was neatly buttoned and sported a string necktie; his felt hat was not peaked to shed rain, but had a thin crease that ran parallel to the brim around the crown, and the top was flattened, California-style. His boots showed the rub of stirrup-wear, but had flat heels. More telling than anything else was the buscadero rig around his waist, a cartridge belt supporting twin holsters that held a pair of old Army Colts. His grip on the Spencer carbine with which he was covering them seemed casual, but its muzzle was rock-steady.

"You can put the gun down, Toland," Dave said calmly. "You know who I am, and that I got as much business here as you have."

"I never seen them two," Toland said. "Who're they?"

"Friends of mine," Clemson told him curtly. "That's all you need to know."

Toland stared at Jessie. He said challengingly, "How about you . . ." He saw Jessie's lips compressing angrily, and tried to meet the direct stare she now focused on him with her green eyes. ". . . lady," he said grudgingly. Then he went on, "You feel like introducing yourself, seeing as how Dave ain't going to?"

"Not that it's any business of yours, but my name is Jessica Starbuck. And my friend's name is Ki," Jessica replied coldly.

"Starbuck," Toland frowned. "I've heard that name . . . Oh, hell, I recall now! You're the one Dave used to foreman for down in Southwest Texas! Sorta off your home range, ain't you?"

Dave broke in angrily, "We've had enough of your fooling around, playing like you amount to something, Toland! Now drop the muzzle of that carbine before I take it away from you and ram it down your gullet!"

"Well now," Toland said, a mocking grin spreading over his face. "You know, I clean forgot I was holding this old Spencer." He lowered the butt of the Spencer and looked at Dave. "You and your friends doing a little bit of spying? What in hell is there in that shacktown that's got you interested?"

"I'm not figuring to get into your line of work, if that's what's got you concerned," Dave replied. He explained to Jessie and Ki, "Toland was a wolfer a while back, and I hired him to get rid of a passel of calf-killing lobos that was on the C-Dot range when I took it over. He was a right good wolfer, but now I hear he's begun bounty hunting. You doing all right in your new work, Toland?"

Toland grinned like the wolves he'd once trapped. "Between the Nation and No Man's Land, I'm making out all right, Clemson. A sight better'n you are, I'd imagine. Now I'm going to ask you, polite as I know how, to tell me why you're prowling around here."

"I'm looking for my stepdaughter," Dave answered curtly.

"That'd be the one named Retha?"

"You know just as well as you know her name that she's the only stepdaughter I've got."

"What give you the idea of looking here?" Toland asked.

"She was supposed to come up to my line camp yesterday, but didn't. I figured she might've stopped off to visit down there in the settlement."

"That's an unlikely story, Clemson! If she—"

Dave broke in on the bounty hunter. "Unlikely or not, we just saw her down there. And now, if you'll step aside, we'll go about our business and you can go back to minding yours."

An idea had been brewing in Jessie's quick mind. She said, "Dave, wait just a minute." She turned to

Toland. "Your business is hunting wanted men. I suppose you've gone through these hills at one time or another?"

"Sure. I've wolfed in 'em and I've hunted bigger game in 'em lately. Why? You got somebody you want brought in?"

"No. But surely you'd know them well enough to guide Ki and me around them and show us what they're like."

Under his breath, Ki said warningly, "Jessie!"

Jessie shook her head and went on, "I don't expect you to work for nothing. I'll pay you a fair price."

"Why'd you want me to guide you around? The Quartzes ain't all that big so you'd get lost in 'em."

"Why I want you to is none of your affair, Toland," Jessie replied crisply. "Do you want the job, or don't you?"

"Well now, since your name's Starbuck, you can afford to pay pretty good, if what I heard about you from Dave is the truth," Toland said slowly. "I guess we can make a dicker. I ain't got much time to put in, but it won't take very long."

"What do you call a long time?" Jessie asked. "Two days? Three days?"

"Why, Miss Starbuck, the Quartzes don't stretch much over six or seven miles long and two or three wide. If you just want a quick look-see without stopping too much, we can ride the main trails in what's left of the day. I'll sorta tell you about the side-trails, and if you wanta take any of 'em, you can come back later and poke around on your own."

Jessie turned to Dave Clemson and said, "Dave, I'm assuming that you intend to go down to the settlement and talk to Retha . . ."

When Jessie's voice trailed off questioningly, Dave said, "Why, sure, Jessie. That's the reason we're here."

"Don't you think it'd be better if you talked to her alone?" Jessie asked. "If Ki and I went along, she might resent our being brought into something that's really your own family matter."

"I hadn't stopped to think about that," Clemson replied with a thoughtful frown. "I'm not sure but what you're right. I don't want to cut you and Ki loose, though."

"You wouldn't be cutting us loose," Jessie said. "If we do engage Mr. Toland as a guide, I'm sure he'd consider it part of his obligation to see that we got back to the prairie. Once we know which direction to ride to find the C-Dot, we won't have any trouble getting there."

"Oh, I'd sure get you headed right," Toland put in.

"What would you consider a fair fee for guiding us the rest of the day?" Jessie asked him.

"Oh, I ain't out to gouge nobody, Miss Starbuck. How does fifty dollars sound to you?"

"It sounds like a lot more money than you can possibly earn in a half-day, but I won't dicker with you. I'll pay that much," Jessie replied.

"If it's settled, then, we can start whenever you say. This is as good a place to leave from as any," the bounty hunter suggested.

"Dave?" Jessie asked Clemson.

"Why sure, if that's what you want to do, Jessie," he said. "The more I think about it, the better I like the idea of having a private talk with Retha."

"I'm sure it's a good idea," Jessie assured him. "You go on and find her, Dave. We'll be back late, so don't wait supper for us, but if Nettie would leave something on the kitchen table for us to eat when we get there—"

"Don't worry, Jessie. I'll see to it," Dave replied.

After his first word of warning, Ki had not protested, nor did his face show any emotion while Jessie completed the deal with Toland. After Clemson had ridden away, he said, "We have a full canteen, Toland, but I hope there are creeks or springs in the hills, where we can water our horses."

"There's a few. Not many, but I know where to fine 'em," Toland replied. He looked at Jessie. "Well, I'm ready to start as soon as . . ." He extended his hand, palm up.

"Ki, will you please pay Mr. Toland?" Jessie said.

Ki fished in the pocket where he carried their traveling funds, and with his fingertips found two double eagles and an eagle. He handed them to Toland. The bounty hunter winked at Jessie as he took the money.

"Smart idea, Miss Starbuck," he said. "Have your China boy carry the money. Nobody'd suspect you'd trust a lot of cash to a servant, they'd figure you'd be the one to rob."

"Ki is neither Chinese nor a servant," Jessie informed Toland, her voice icy. "He is my friend and companion."

His voice showing his confusion, Toland asked plaintively, "Now how was I to know that? But I'll remember it, I sure will."

They set out on their tour, and for the next three hours the bounty hunter led them along paths that showed little evidence of use, riding into the lower range of hills that stood south of Outlaw Mountain, and circling through canyons where the only signs of past habitation were occasional heaps consisting of a few boards, all that remained of a cabin or shack.

Toland seemed to be relieved after Dave Clemson left them. His voice lost its harsh overtone and he talked quite volubly. He did not quite discard his air of braggadocio, though. He pointed out two spots where he claimed he'd captured wanted men, explaining that there had once been more cabins, but as these had fallen into disuse, their lumber was taken by the settlement dwellers.

As their trip continued, they encountered huge areas where the grayish soil seemed to sparkle from within, and Toland told them that the little formation of hills had gotten its name from the quartz flakes its soil contained, and from the occasional outcrops of pure quartz that were to be found on the hillsides. He indicated sunken rectangles that marked old graves, and pointed out the fire-pits left by Kiowas and Comanches, explaining how to tell one from the other. Once he showed them the broken tipi poles beside a dry water hole that he said had been a regular buffalo camp for the Comanches.

Water was scarce; that was apparent to both Jessie and Ki as they rode along the courses of dried-up creeks and went past the cracked and sere hollows that had once been water holes. They saw a few trickling streams not much wider than an outspread palm, and in one place a pool of clean water formed by a spring.

Jessie had let Toland do the talking, only infrequently interrupting his monologue with a question. Now, as they stopped at the water hole to let the horses drink, she asked him, "What caused the water to dry up? There are a lot of creekbeds and holes where there used to be springs."

"Earthquake, way before I ever come here," he replied. "It's worse now for water than it was then, but some of them little cricks took a long time to go dry."

As the sun slanted lower and lower, Toland led them in a wide sweep back to their starting point. The dim trail led past Outlaw Mountain, and occasionally a hill jutting out from the base took them up on the side of the big rise itself.

"Is it true that this is still used by outlaws for a hideout?" Jessie asked, looking up the steep slope along which they rode.

"Not since the water give out," Toland said unhesitatingly. "It used to be, I guess, or it wouldn't of been called Outlaw Mountain."

They reached the base of the big rise, and Toland led them around the foothills that extended from its flanks. The sun was just touching the horizon when he reined in and pointed.

"Now keep shifting a little to the south of where the sun's going down, and that'll put you to the C-Dot a little bit after dark," he told them. "I'd ride a ways with you, but I got to take a couple of packmules from the settlement up to Fort Supply tomorrow to bring back some truck for the store."

"How long a trip is that?" Ki asked.

"I figure two days to go, four to come back with the load. But it's pretty much level country, it ain't a bad ride."

"You've surprised me very pleasantly, Mr. Toland," Jessie said, hiding her distaste for the man. "You've been a very good guide. Thank you. We'll find our way from here, I'm sure."

Toland touched his hat and rode off toward the trail that led to the settlement. Ki touched his roan's ribs with his toe, but reined in when Jessie said, "Dismount and act like you're tightening your cinch, Ki. Hurry!"

Without hesitation, Ki swung to the ground and busied himself behind the horse. Looking up at Jessie, he saw that her eyes were following Toland.

"You saw something in the Quartz Mountains that you want to look at a second time," Ki said after a moment's thought.

"If that's a guess, it's a good one, Ki. If you thought it out, it's a good deduction." Jessie was still watching Toland. As soon as the bounty hunter disappeared behind the first rise of the foothills, she said, "All right. There's not much chance he'll come back. Let's go, Ki."

90

Ki mounted. Jessie reined Sun around and led the way back in the direction from which they'd just come. Ki got a belated start, but sped up the gelding with a nudge of his heel.

"Please satisfy my curiosity, Jessie," he said as he came abreast of her. "We both looked at the same places. What did you see that I missed?"

"A trail, Ki. A trail where Toland said there wasn't any, along the side of Outlaw Mountain. It was almost invisible, and there's a chance I'm mistaken, but if I'm not, Toland lied to us. I intend to find out why."

"He's not a man who'd forget something like that, especially when you'd asked him about an outlaw hideout on the mountain," Ki said thoughtfully.

"No. And if you remember, while we were on the trail that took us a little way up the mountain, he pointed out things in the opposite direction, things that weren't at all important."

Ki looked at the sky. The dark blue of dusk was shading the eastern horizon, though behind them the earth's rim was just beginning to bite off the sun.

"It's getting late," he pointed out. "Would we be better off going back to the C-Dot tonight and starting out fresh in the morning?"

"We're here right now, Ki, and the location of that place where I thought I saw a trail is still fresh in my mind."

"That's the answer, then," Ki nodded. "You're right."

They pushed on. When they reached the hump where the low hill extending from the base of Outlaw Mountain forced the trail to loop up the mountain's flank, Jessie reined in.

"That trail I saw, or thought I saw, was on the other side of that hump," she frowned. "But the light's changed since we were here. I don't see it now."

"Let's move ahead a step at a time," Ki suggested. "Maybe it's only visible from a certain place, or from only one angle."

Inching Sun ahead, Jessie kept her eyes fixed on the ground ahead of them. The soil covering the flanks of Outlaw Mountain lay thin and patchy over an underlying stratum of shale-like rock. The rock was in layers, chipped and broken at the edges where layer overlapped layer. It was in the short stretches of these overlaps that the dirt had collected, blown by winds, washed there from higher up by the infrequent rains.

There was no grass growing on the baked soil of the area they were searching, just an occasional clump of coonberry and buckbrush. The light was fading rapidly now, though, and Jessie had to strain her eyes in the gathering darkness as they moved slowly forward. They reached the top of the hump before her memory meshed and she recalled the stretch of ground that lay just ahead of them. At the same time she saw what had caught her eye earlier.

"There it is!" she told Ki, pointing at a broken clod of earth that rose a scant few inches above what appeared to be undisturbed ground, a dozen feet ahead of them. "Do you see it?"

Ki leaned toward her from his saddle to follow with his eyes the line of Jessie's pointing finger. He studied the clod for a few moments, then said, "It looks to me as though a horse's hoof has cut a groove in that hunk of dirt."

"Exactly!" Jessie exclaimed, satisfaction in her voice. "Let's take a closer look."

Dismounting, they walked slowly up to the protruding chunk of dirt that had caught Jessie's eye. They bent over it for a close inspection. The clod of earth stood alone, rising from the level, stone-hard surface of the barren ground. The groove that had caught Jessie's quick eyes was clean-cut, a smooth-sided oval indentation scored from top to bottom. At the bottom of the groove, the soil was packed hard. Jessie bent over the mark.

"I'm right, Ki," she said. "I can see the line of a horseshoe inside the groove, at the bottom."

"There's no question about it," Ki agreed after he'd given the mark a close look. He took a pinch of dirt from one side of the clod and rubbed it between his thumb and forefinger. The dry earth crumbled to fine dust at his lightest touch. "This soil is so dry that it wouldn't hold that print very long. A day or two, I'd guess."

"Why would someone on a horse by leaving the trail—such as it is—and going up the side of this mountain unless they had a reason, Ki? And what reason could they have?"

"There's only one that I can think of," he replied.

"Let's leave the horses here and go on a little farther," Jessie suggested. "Even as hard as this ground is, a horse going over it must have left some more prints."

Ki looked at the sky. The light was going fast now. In the west, the setting sun was giving out its last red glow, and the blue above their heads was deepening into purple. Ki shook his head.

"We'd better wait until morning, Jessie. If we go blundering around up here without being able to see clearly, we might destroy any other prints that are ahead of us," he pointed out.

Jessie hesitated, then nodded agreement. "I suppose so. If we leave now, there'll still be enough light to see the trail to that water hole where we stopped this afternoon. If I remember, it's not much more than a mile from here."

"If we're going to stay very long, the horses will need water," Ki said thoughtfully. "And it would be as safe a place as any to leave them while we're looking around tomorrow."

"It would be better than riding to the C-Dot and back. And a night on the ground won't hurt us."

"Dave's going to wonder why we didn't get back," Ki said as they reached the horses and mounted.

"He'll just think we got back late from the ride with Toland and didn't feel like going on to the ranch in the dark." Jessie paused thoughtfully, then said, "I had a feeling when we were with him that Toland was trying not to show us things he didn't want us to see. Ki, there's something going on here on Outlaw Mountain. And I don't intend to stop looking until we've found out what it is!"

★

Chapter 9

Dusk was heavy with night's arrival when Jessie and Ki reached the water hole that Toland had showed them earlier in the day. They made a dark camp—a simple camp, since they had no bedrolls, cooking utensils, or any food to cook. Ki and Jessie each carried a salt sack containing some parched corn and strips of jerky in their saddlebags, so they did not face going to bed hungry.

Darkness was complete by the time they'd unsaddled and had a few bites of their emergency rations. Leaning against their saddles, they looked up at the stars, just beginning to show clear as the light night breeze carried away the last of the days' heat haze. The night was utterly still; not a bird call or the scurrying of an animal broke the silence that now settled over the little clearing around the waterhole.

"I'm not sure we were right to leave that trail, Ki," Jessie said in the darkness.

"We talked about it and decided that if we tried to follow it in the dark, we might destroy what little sign there is."

"I know. But we could leave the horses here and climb up on Outlaw Mountain above the trail. We know it must lead around the side of the mountain."

"We only *think* we know. Suppose the trail turns uphill? We could miss it in the dark and blunder our way into trouble."

"If there is an outlaw hideout there, it would be easier to spot from a distance in the dark than it would be by daylight. They'd need a fire to cook with."

"Fires make smoke, Jessie, and we can see smoke more easily in the daylight than we could see the glow of a fire at night."

"I guess there's something to be said on both sides," Jessie agreed. She stretched and yawned. "I'm going to sleep, then. We'll see what we turn up tomorrow."

Ki woke suddenly in the darkness. He lay quietly, wondering why he'd awakened and what was bothering him now that he was awake. The breeze had died while he slept, and the sparse, ground-hugging brush was not the kind that broke the quiet with rustling leaves, even when the wind was brisk. His first thought was that one of the horses might have whinnied, and he looked toward the water hole. The two animals stood where they'd been tethered, the light bulk of Sun beside the darker form of the roan. Both were motionless in the starlight.

Suddenly, Ki realized that the source of his uneasiness wasn't what he might have heard, but what he was *not* hearing. There was no sound of Jessie's breathing from the spot where she'd lain down when they turned in.

Straining his eyes through the gloom, Ki could see the outline of her saddle, but Jessie was gone. He lay still for a few seconds, thinking that she might have stepped away from their sleeping place a short distance to relieve herself. There was no noise at all. Rolling to his feet, Ki stepped over to Jessie's saddle. The ground where she'd been lying was cool. He looked around. Her rifle, still in its scabbard, lay beside the saddle, but her gunbelt was gone.

Knowing that Jessie had inherited a strong strain of the Starbuck stubbornness that had made Alex so successful, Ki needed no clues to deduce at once what had happened. He himself had trained Jessie to move with the silence and stealth of a *ninja,* one of those legendary Japanese warriors who could steal up on even a watchful enemy with such skill that they seemed to materialize from nowhere.

Ki knew that if Jessie's Colt was gone, it was in its holster on Jessie's hip, and that she had gone alone to look for the hideout, which they were both convinced by now must be somewhere on Outlaw Mountain. He wasted no time. Going to his saddle, Ki unfolded his leather vest and slipped it on, wound his *surushin* around his waist, and slid his feet into his rope-soled slippers. He left the camp and started at a fast dogtrot back along the trail they'd followed to the water hole.

On their way from Outlaw Mountain to their campsite, Ki had glanced back frequently, noting details along the trail that might be useful in finding their way when they returned. Though darkness obscured some of the landmarks he'd stored in his memory, and the changing light gave others a different aspect, he had no trouble in finding the winding way that led back to the spot where Jessie had seen the hoofprint.

He stopped there for a moment, trying to decide what he'd do if he were Jessie. Remembering her remark about going a short distance up the mountainside and working around it from the point where the hoofprint had been made, Ki started up the slope. It was not precipitous, but it was steep enough to force him to lean forward to keep his balance. A dozen feet above the hoofprint, he turned and headed east.

While the ground in the Quartzes was generally barren, Ki soon found that the surface of Outlaw Mountain was totally bald. He also discovered that walking around the slanting mountainside was not really difficult. There were stretches of loose shale and patches of gullied, crumbling earth that were treacherous under his feet, but there were also areas where the bedrock that formed the mountain's core provided solid footing.

He did not hurry. He knew Jessie was ahead of him, but he counted on her moving more slowly than he was doing. He had a mental picture of her feeling her way, stopping now and then to listen and to peer through the starlight.

As Ki moved farther and farther around the mountainside, the character of the surface began to change. The loose dirt and layers of crumbling shale petered out and vanished as he made his way through a wide area strewn with massive boulders. Some of the great stones were the size of a man, but even more of them were bigger than a horse, and a few ranged up the size of a small house. Even in the faint starshine, Ki could see the glint of quartz crystals embedded in the granite of the huge rocks.

Beyond the boulders, Ki found that the stone core of Outlaw Mountain had been laid bare. On this portion of the eastern slope, there was only solid rock underfoot. The slant was steeper, the footing more treacherous.

Ki was forced to move more slowly. He was growing anxious now, as he still had not caught up with Jessie. He began to wonder whether he'd been mistaken in his deductions, whether Jessie had indeed gone out to explore the mountain as he'd thought, or whether she'd awakened, felt restless, and strolled only a short way from camp.

He was getting ready to turn back when a flash of light shot up from nowhere ahead of him. The light flickered along the ground for a moment, then vanished. When his surprise at seeing the unexpected phenomenon ebbed, Ki realized that what he'd seen was the flame from a match struck to light a cigar or pipe by someone in a canyon a short distance in front of him. Silently, cautiously, he crept forward.

Ahead, Ki saw a wide swath of total blackness, and recognized it as the lip of a canyon. He dropped to all fours and inched on his hands and knees across the bare rock surface to the canyon's edge. Dropping prone, he wriggled silently forward until he could peer over the canyon's edge.

Below him on the floor of the canyon, the man who had lighted the cigar puffed at it. In the deep gloom where the starshine did not reach, the tip of the cigar lighted the man's face and the area around him as effectively as a lantern.

Ki could not see the smoker's face, for the broad brim of the man's hat shielded it. He could see that the smoker was sitting on a boulder, leaning back against the sheer rock wall. His cigar was clamped in his mouth, and between his legs he held the barrel of a rifle, its butt resting on the canyon floor.

For a moment, Ki watched silently. There was no doubt in his mind what he'd stumbled onto. The canyon must lead to a wider canyon that cut into Outlaw Mountain. The man could be nothing other than a sentry on lookout duty, and there was but one job that would keep him in the canyon in the dead of night, alone. The man must be guarding the canyon, which could only be the entrance to the hideout that no one was sure existed, the hideout that had given the mountain its name.

Watching the sentry, Ki debated only briefly. Farther up the canyon, there must be enough outlaws to enable them to keep a guard on duty all night at the entrance. It would be easy enough to capture the lone sentry, but such a move would be pointless and foolhardy.

This was a time, Ki saw, when he should not act alone, when even he and Jessie together would not be wise in attacking the hideout.

Edging back from the canyon rim, he stood up and started moving silently away. In the darkness he did not see the ledge of rock that rose in his path. His slippered toe struck hard against the ledge, a cruelly painful blow.

Ki threw out his arms, flailing them to regain his balance. His foot slipped on the smooth surface under it. Ki felt himself falling backward. He tried to throw his body forward, but the stone underfoot was too slick. He tumbled and fell. As he bent forward, his head struck the high ledge that had tripped him.

On his back, Ki slid the few feet to the canyon rim. The noise of his fall had alerted the guard. Ki heard the man shout, heard the blast of his rifle as he fired.

Then Ki was falling from the canyon rim. He brought his body back under his control, twisting it in midair to bring his legs down, to land catlike on his feet. He had almost succeeded in regaining his balance when the sentry fired again. A searing pain burst in Ki's head and he knew nothing more.

Jessie was fifty yards up the canyon from Ki when the rifle shot shattered the night's stillness.

She had slept only briefly, tossed restlessly, awakened suddenly, and lain quietly on the hard earth, looking up at the stars, willing herself to go back to sleep. Usually, Jessie could obey her own command, but tonight she could not. At the instant she awoke, her mind began weaving together the threads that had been dangling in her subconscious mind.

Suddenly it all formed a pattern: Dave Clemson's letter, the attack in San Antonio, Dave's story, his suspicions, the unsettled situation in Greer County that opened the way for it to be taken over by the lawless cartel,

Toland's sudden and still unexplained appearance, the bounty hunter's avoidance of Outlaw Mountain, the hoofprint on a seldom-used trail...

It was a pattern Jessie did not like. She stood up, knowing she could not sleep until she'd tired her muscles. Ki slept placidly, his head on his saddle. Jessie buckled on her Colt, picked up her boots, and walked silently on bare feet over the rough ground until she was far enough from the water hole to be sure that the grating of her boot soles would not rouse Ki. Then she'd started for Outlaw Mountain.

She'd moved much more slowly than Ki, for, after finding the hoofprint in the clod of dirt, she had walked along the mountain's flank in a straight line from the hoofprint. Her progress had been a matter of inching along, stopping after every step or two and bending close to the ground, looking for more signs in the soft earth that someone had passed that way recently.

A quarter-mile from where she'd started, there was a place where the soil had been disturbed. Jessie stirred the area with her boot toe and uncovered a still-moist clod of horse manure. The condition of the earth showed that the rider had taken time to stop and cover the evidence of his passing.

Encouraged, Jessie had moved ahead. The starlight had been bright enough for her to see the mouth of the canyon yawning ahead. She'd stopped and debated silently, deciding finally that it would be foolish to enter it in the darkness, though its location indicated that the canyon had been the place the rider had been heading for.

Instead of going into the black opening that yawned in the solid rock of the mountainside, Jessie had climbed the slope. She had stayed as far from the canyon as possible as she climbed, but kept its near rim in sight. Her progress had taken her beyond the point where the

101

sentry kept watch, and she had been standing away from the rim, trying to decide whether to go farther up the mountainside before approaching the rim, when she'd heard the shot fired by the guard.

Instead of rushing toward the sound, Jessie stood still. A few moments after the echoes of the rifle blast died away, light showed from the head of the canyon. Jessie crept close enough to the rim to get a glimpse of its floor. Three men, one carrying a lantern, all three carrying rifles, were running toward the canyon's mouth.

Jessie drew back from the rim and paralleled their course until the light stopped. She crept up to the rim again and looked down. When she saw Ki lying on the canyon floor, his head bleeding, Jessie drew her Colt. There were only four men, and she had five shells in the revolver.

She held her fire when one of the men said loudly, "Ah, shit! He ain't hurt bad. Your slug just grazed his head, Slim."

"It's a damn wonder I hit him at all," the sentry said. "I heard a little noise and seen him dancing like a wild man up on the edge there, and let off a miss. Then he begun tumbling down, and I guess I winged him on the fly."

When Jessie heard the canyon rim mentioned and saw the sentry gesture toward the spot where she was crouched, she dropped flat. When the man holding the lantern lifted it and peered up, trying to see past the ring of light into the darkness, the shadow of the canyon's lip hid her.

"I'd give a whole hell of a lot to know why somebody was prowling around here at this time of night," the lantern-carrier said. He stepped over to where Ki lay and put the lantern down, then bent over to get a close look at Ki's face.

"Who in hell is he?" one of the others asked.

"I don't know who he is," the man with the lantern

replied. "He ain't got a gun, and no knife, either." He felt Ki's vest pockets and announced, "Nothing in his pockets but some pieces of cut-up tin. And I'll be god-damned if he ain't some kinda yellow-bellied China-man!"

One of the others guffawed. "Well, by God, he come to the wrong place if he figures we're gonna hire him to do our washing. He ain't nowhere near as good to look at as that little washerwoman we got now!"

"Shut up, Batters!" snapped the man holding the lantern. "If you think it's funny to have somebody walk up on our hideout, you're riding with the wrong bunch!"

"No offense, Perk," the joker said quickly. "I didn't mean nothing by what I said."

"All right," Perk said. "You and Granger pick him up and lug him back to camp. Something like this, I got to talk to Toland about."

Jessie was not too surprised to hear the bounty hunter's name mentioned by the outlaw. It simply confirmed her earlier feeling. Perk's voice drew her attention back to the canyon.

"You hear anything before the Chink jumped up and you seen him?" he was asking Slim.

"Not a thing. I was just setting back, wishing I was over to Mobeetie, in bed with that redhead at Mabel's place, and all of a sudden, there he was." The outlaw paused for a moment and went on, "I know you told me not to shoot, Perk, but honest to God, I was so took by surprise that I just cut loose before I thought."

"You done right," Perk assured the guard. He saw that the other two men were waiting, holding Ki's limp form, and picked up the lantern. To Slim, he added. "You keep your eyes sharp the rest of the night, you hear? No telling how many more of them Chinamen is prowling around out on the mountain."

Jessie let Perk and the men who were carrying Ki get

103

ahead of her a few yards before she slipped away and followed them along the canyon rim. She did not have to get close or take special care to move silently, for the lantern light outlined the rim, and the scraping of the trio's boots on the stone floor covered any small noises she might make.

For a hundred yards or more the canyon ran string-straight, then Jessie saw the light turning away in front of her. She stopped quickly, waiting until it was safe to move again, intending to cut across the curve and continue following Perk and his men. Her heart sank when the light disappeared; she was afraid they had gone into a cave that would be impossible for her to enter. Then the light reappeared, paler now, outlining the rim of a solid wall that extended in a rough circle, its ends at each side lost in the blackness.

Moving cautiously, she started toward the glow. She reached the point where the light had vanished, and there she learned why it had seemed to go out. The canyon wall there was bridged by a stone arch, thirty or forty feet thick. Beyond the arch, the canyon widened out into a sort of crater. Jessie stole up to its rim and looked down.

At her feet a box canyon opened. Jessie guessed that the canyon was more than a hundred yards across. She could estimate its size only by the faint, intermittent sparkling of the quartz crystals imbedded in the canyon walls as they caught the rays from the small pool of lantern light and threw them back in tiny sparkles. The portion of the wall that she could by the lantern's beams seemed to be of the same stone that formed the sides of the canyon, and were just as sheerly vertical. Around the walls, tarpaulins had been stretched on corner poles to form crude, tentlike shelters. Horses were crowded into a rope corral at one side of the big enclosure, and a small spring made little pond near the center.

There were a dozen or more men milling around on the floor of the canyon, their voices mingling in an excited babble that made it impossible for Jessie to distinguish a single voice or to hear what was being said. As the men moved around, she got an occasional glimpse of Ki. The men who carried him in had laid him on the canyon floor. Standing beside Ki's still form was the man called Perk, talking with Skip Toland.

Slowly the babble of voices died away, and Jessie could hear what was being said.

". . . and that damn Starbuck woman can't be far off. I done my best to steer 'em away from this place when I was showing 'em around earlier. Figured it was better for me to do the guiding than to let 'em find somebody that didn't know better'n to show 'em this hole along with everything else."

"What're you gonna do about her, Skip?" Perk asked. "The Chink don't matter now, we got him."

"See you hold on to him," Toland warned, "And whatever he is, he ain't a Chink. Not that it makes much difference."

"But the woman—" Perk began.

Toland interrupted him. "I ain't got time to do anything about her. I told you I got to get to Fort Supply. There's an order of ammunition I got to pick up; you'll need a lot more'n you got, before this is over. And you told me yesterday you're running low on grub and whiskey."

"How long you figure to be gone?" Perk asked.

"Two days to go up, four to come back, because the mules can't go no faster loaded."

"You never did say what you want us to do about the woman," Perk reminded Toland.

"Dammit, Perk, you *know* what! You men scatter out at daylight and track her down. There ain't much she can do by herself."

"What'll we do when we find her?" one of the men asked.

"Grab her and bring her here to the hideout," Toland said. "Hold on to her till I get back."

"How about us having some fun with her?" one of the men in the group called.

Toland's voice was cold and merciless as he replied, "There's only two things I'll tell you not to do. Keep her alive and don't bust up her hands, because the boss has got a lot of papers to make her sign. And I guess you're smart enough to figure out what that means."

★

Chapter 10

Jessie's hand went instinctively to her Colt when she heard the bounty hunter's words, but in spite of the temptation she did not draw and fire. At that range the Colt would not be accurate enough for her to be sure of getting Toland with her first shot. The gesture also reminded her that Toland was Ki's insurance. As long as the bounty hunter held command, the outlaws would obey his orders. For the moment, her own danger was greater than Ki's; she must stay alive and free if both of them were to survive.

Calmly, Jessie took stock of her situation. She was neither worried nor afraid. She sympathized with Ki as she watched two of the outlaws bind his hands and feet and carry him to one of the tarpaulin shelters, but she knew there was nothing she could do to help him at the moment. Though Ki might be uncomfortable until the bounty hunter returned, she was sure he'd be safe.

Even if he was safe, however, Jessie was well aware that she was not. There were no hiding places in the barren Quartz Mountains where she could be sure to elude more than a dozen cutthroats when they scattered at daybreak and began searching for her, and daybreak could not be far away. Common sense urged her to hurry back to the water hole, take the horses, and get out of reach, but she disregarded common sense for the moment and held her precarious position long enough to study the box canyon.

It was a formidable fortress. As nearly as she could tell in the darkness, there were no hand or footholds by which the canyon walls could be climbed, either up or down. No ledges ran from the rim to the canyon floor. At no place around the rim was there a bush or tree or boulder to shelter a rifleman firing down into the canyon, while the outlaws defending it would have a clear view of anyone posted along the rim.

Jessie counted the outlaws. They had scattered now, but she had no trouble getting an accurate tally. There were fourteen of them, not counting Toland, who had gotten his horse from the rope corral and was holding its reins as he talked to Perk and two of the others.

Fifteen lawless men, to which number Toland would quite probably add a few more, combined with the cartel's resources in leadership, weaponry, and money, would be a force large enough to seize control of an area much bigger and more thickly populated than Greer County. The thought spurred her to action. She moved stealthily along the rim to the stone arch that framed the canyon mouth.

Like the box canyon itself, the entrance was easy to defend. A dozen experienced fighters could defend it successfully against any force smaller than an army company backed up by an artillery battery. The arch, which was the canyon's only entrance, was a frame of solid stone. At its center it rose high enough to allow a man on horseback to ride through without having to duck, and it was wide enough to allow three riders to enter it abreast.

At the top, the arch was at least thirty feet thick, and riflemen sheltering behind its jutting sides had a clear field of fire for fifty or sixty yards down the canyon that was the only way to approach the hideout. With a sentry posted below the curve in the canyon to warn them, the outlaws could be ready to fight off any force that might attack them.

While Jessie was still studying the canyon's layout, Toland mounted and rode out through the arch. Jessie watched the renegades for a few minutes longer, to give Toland time to get ahead of her. The men in the canyon were gathering around Perk, and from his gestures Jessie could tell that he was dividing them up and assigning them to areas in anticipation of the search that would begin soon. It was time for her to go. Stealing away from the canyon rim, Jessie hurried down the mountain's flank and started for the water hole.

Consciousness returned to Ki slowly until he tried to move his hands. When they did not respond, his mind snapped alert and he remembered losing his balance on the canyon rim, hearing a shot, and beginning to topple backward. He shook his head, and a sharp flash of pain darted through his body.

Ki knew then that he'd been wounded. In spite of the pain, he twisted around, testing the ropes that held his arms and legs. The outlaws had done a good job of binding him. The ropes that immobilized him had no give to them, and Ki let himself relax. His head was sore, and his face was stiff with dried, crusted blood. Ignoring the pain, Ki twisted his body to look across the floor of the box canyon.

Except for the light shed by the lantern, which still stood on the ground, Ki's surroundings were shrouded in darkness. He could see that he was lying under a shelter of some kind, but that was all. There was no sign of Jessie, and Ki wondered what had happened to her. He could surmise what had happened to himself though he still was not quite sure where he was.

He returned his attention to the circle of light where Perk stood with the outlaws clustered around him. He could see from their attitudes that Perk must be in charge of the band, and that he was giving the men orders or instructions.

Ki's sixth sense told him that the orders had some connection with himself and Jessie. The outlaws began to scatter, and Perk confirmed what Ki had only been able to guess.

"Batters!" the leader called, and one of the men who had been walking toward the tarpaulin where Ki lay turned to look back. "Batters, you better take a look at the Chink or Jap or whatever he is. Toland said hold on to him, and from what I hear, them yellowbellies is slicker'n possum fat!"

Ki closed his eyes and feigned unconsciousness as Batters came to where he lay. He felt the outlaw's hands running over the ropes that bound his wrists and feet.

Batters straightened up and called to Perk, "He ain't come to yet, Perk. He's tied good enough to hold him, though."

"All right," Perk replied. "Slim's gonna stay here, he's been up guarding all night. And I'll leave Fat Joe to take Slim's place up the canyon. Neither one of 'em would be much good looking for the woman."

Even with his eyes closed, Ki learned a great deal that he hadn't known before. He'd already deduced that he was in the hideout that no one would admit existed on Outlaw Mountain. He knew that somehow Toland had come to be in command of the renegades. Most important, he'd learned that Jessie was still free and that the gang was going out to look for her, leaving only two men behind as guards.

If he needed any further confirmation that a search for Jessie was about to begin, Ki got it when he heard the *snick-snick* of metal rubbing metal as Batters loaded fresh shells into the magazine of a rifle or carbine. Then he heard a grunt of satisfaction as the outlaw finished his job, followed by the grating of boot soles as Batters left to join the others.

With Batters gone, Ki felt free to watch again. Soft gray dawn light was beginning to seep into the box canyon by now, and a breakfast fire had been kindled. Between the flickering of the small blaze and the brightening of dawn into sunrise, Ki could see well enough. He watched the outlaws as they ate hurriedly before bringing out their horses and saddling up.

By the time they were ready to ride out, there was enough light to enable him to follow their progress to the stone arch, which he saw clearly now for the first time. The entryway gave Ki the last clue he needed to orient himself. As though he'd walked over the ground, observing it, or studied it on a large-scale map, Ki knew almost exactly where he was.

He watched Slim as the night guard crawled into his blankets under one of the other tarpaulin shelters, and when he was quite sure the outlaw had gone to sleep, Ki began to test his bonds again. They still resisted all his efforts to slip free. Ki fought them until his head started to ache again, then resigned himself to remaining a captive for a while and went to sleep.

Ki usually slept like a cat, woke as quickly, and was as instantly alert. Reaction from his head wound made a difference this time. When the beginning of awareness came to him, he did not open his eyes. His head was throbbing, his hands and feet were numb from his bonds. The ropes hurt more than the pounding in his head, and without opening his eyes, Ki began struggling to free himself while he was still only half awake. Dimly and indistinctly he heard a voice calling him from far off.

For several moments Ki did not respond to the call. Then he heard his name repeated again, clearly this time, and knew it must be Jessie calling. He tried to speak as he struggled to open his eyes, but a hand pressed his mouth closed. Then his eyes opened and he blinked in the daylight and saw Bright Sunrise kneeling beside him bending over him.

"Be quiet, Ki," the Arapaho girl whispered when she saw his eyes open. "I will take my hand away, but you must whisper."

Ki nodded his understanding, ignoring the pain that resulted when he moved his head. Bright Sunrise removed her hand.

"What are you doing here?" he asked. "You should be at the ranch."

Bright Sunrise shook her head. "My work there is finished until next week. Now I have come to work here for a while."

"But these men are outlaws!" Ki protested.

"So are many of my people, Ki. We are used to being outlaws to the whites," she said, her voice sad. "I do not fight for these men, I do not fight for Mrs. Clemson or her husband. I do my work and ask no questions. Now lie still for a moment. You have much blood on your face. I will get water and wash it away, then you will feel better."

Bright Sunrise got to her feet and left. Ki lay quietly thoughtful. During the years he'd spent in the West, first with Alex Starbuck and later with Jessie, he'd learned a bit about Indian logic. In some cases it was very closely akin to that of the Orient, and to whites, both seemed illogical. Given the relationship between the Indian tribes and the whites, Ki decided her answers had been reasonable. Bright Sunrise returned with a damp cloth and bathed Ki's face. Getting rid of the caked blood relieved him more than a little.

"Thank you, Bright Sunrise," he said when she'd finished. "You're kind and thoughtful."

"You were kind to me when I was looking at the horse. You did not curse at me or strike me."

"Why should I have? You weren't doing any harm."

"No. But some men would have."

Ki asked the question that had been bothering him. "Does Mrs. Clemson know you work here, Bright Sunrise?"

"Of course not. Why should I tell her? She only cares that I do what she pays me to. I owe her nothing else."

"Do the men here know you work at the C-Dot?"

"One does. Maybe he has told others, I do not know."

"Who is he, Bright Sunrise?" When she did not answer at once, Ki mentioned the name that seemed most logical. "Toland?"

"How did you find that out?"

"It's not important," Ki replied. Then, hoping he could confirm the suspicion he'd formed during the hours he and Jessie had spent with the bounty hunter, he asked, "Toland is part Indian, isn't he?"

She nodded. "His mother was Comanche. He still has family living in the Nation." She looked at Ki, puzzlement on her face. "How do you find out so much in such a little time, Ki? Do your people have medicine that gives you the power to know things?"

Ki only smiled. He knew quite well that Bright Sunrise would not have asked such a question of one of her own people, who considered what they loosely described as "medicine" to be a personal and very private affair. Instead he asked, "Will you untie me, Bright Sunrise?"

For a moment, Bright Sunrise thought silently, then she said slowly, "No. I cannot do that, Ki. It would make much trouble. Toland might even kill me when he comes back."

"Did Toland get you this job?"

"Yes. Why?"

"It doesn't matter." Remembering her education, Ki

decided to try Jesuit logic on the Arapaho girl. He said, "You have two jobs now. Do any of the men here offer you another job?"

"Oh, sure. They say they will pay me to sleep with them. I do not say yes to them, though."

"Would you work for me if I asked you to?"

"Maybe so. What would I do?"

"These ropes on my arms and legs hurt me. I won't ask you again to untie me, but will you loosen them a little?"

"So you can get away?"

"Would it be your fault if I did? Remember," Ki reminded her, "I'm not asking you to untie me, just to loosen the ropes a little bit so they don't hurt me so much."

To Ki's surprise, she said, "I will not do this for pay, Ki. I will do it because it is a debt I owe you."

"You don't owe me anything, Bright Sunrise," Ki frowned. "I've only seen you once before, for a few minutes."

"That one time, when you held me as a captive, I could feel how strong you must be, but you held me gently and let me go when you did not have to. You trusted me with the big horse and did not stay to watch and see that I would keep my promise not to harm him. This is the debt I owe, and we Arapaho pay our debts."

"I still don't think you owe me anything, but I'm not going to argue with you about it," Ki said as Bright Sunrise began to tug at the knots holding his wrists. "And next time we see one another, you won't owe me and I won't owe you, so maybe we can start out then as friends."

"I would like that, Ki. Our people must be kin, and kin must be friends together." Bright Star finished retying the knots around Ki's ankles and stood up. "Now I must do my work. We will talk again later, before I go."

Still not believing his good luck, Ki watched the

Arapaho girl walking across the floor of the canyon. Already, feeling was beginning to return to his hands and feet. He set to work flexing his fingers and wriggling his toes to speed their return to normal while his eyes were busy studying the details of the box canyon and the outlaw camp, looking for a weak spot he could use in the escape he was already planning.

When Jessie reached the water hole, the night was giving up. A line of gray showed in the east, though the canyons between the hills were still ink-black. Saddling both horses quickly, she started for the prairie.

Having left the hideout before Perk began to organize the outlaws' search, she could not be sure of her margin of safety. Mounting Sun and leading the roan, she wound along the trail to the plain. The day brightened after she'd left the hills. Keeping the Quartzes at her back, remembering the direction in which Toland had pointed when the sun was setting the day before, Jessie rode steadily through the brightening morning and reached the ranch less than two hours after sunrise.

Dave Clemson had seen her from a distance, and was pacing back and forth on the veranda when she reined in.

"Where's Ki?" Dave asked. "I hope he ain't—"

"We had a little trouble," Jessie interrupted. "But Ki's safe, at least for a while."

"What the devil happened to you and him?"

"It's a long story, Dave. I'll tell you the whole thing while I eat breakfast. I'm starving. All we had last night was jerky and parched corn, and I nibbled a little jerky while I was riding. But don't worry, we'll work everything out."

"Worry!" Dave exploded. "I was just getting ready to saddle up and go looking for you when I seen you coming across the prairie. I'd have started out last night when

115

you didn't show up, but I didn't figure it'd do you or me much good to go floundering around the Quartzes in the dark, not knowing where to look for you or anything else."

"You did the right thing. You couldn't have helped us much by yourself, even if you'd been able to find us."

"Go on inside, Jessie. Nettie's got your breakfast ready by now; she started it when I told her you was riding up. I'll take care of the horses and be there in a minute."

"Well, you poor little thing!" Nettie exclaimed when Jessie entered the house. "Lost all night, no supper and no breakfast! I'll bet you're starved. Set down, now. I've got a good meal all ready to dish up."

Dave returned to the house before Jessie had finished her meal, and pulled a chair up to the table. He said, "Go on now, tell me what-all happened to you and Ki."

Talking between bites, Jessie gave the Clemsons an abbreviated account of their decision to explore the Quartz Mountains and their discovery of the outlaw hideout.

Because of the many years he'd worked with Alex and then with her, Jessie was ready to give Dave the benefit of the doubt; still, she did not mention her discovery that Skip Toland was the real leader of the outlaw band. She did not include him in her story of what had happened at the box canyon, thus leaving the impression that he'd ridden away from her and Ki before their return to the Quartzes.

When Jessie had finished, Dave said sadly, "Right now I'm sorry I ever wrote you that letter, Jessie. Seems like I just brought you here to get you into a heap of trouble."

"Don't be sorry, Dave. I'd rather face a little trouble now than a lot of trouble later. If the cartel should get control of Greer County and set up a base here, they'd be a lot stronger than they could ever be without it."

116

"I guess you got some kind of plan to go about busting up their scheme?" he asked.

"Right now the only thing I intend to plan is a way to get Ki out of that canyon. You know how important Ki is, Dave."

"Sure. He was Alex's right hand first, now he's yours. What do you want me to do to help, Jessie?"

"It's going to take more than the two of us. Isn't there any law we could look to for help?"

Dave shook his head. "Texas lawmen have got orders not to come in here unless they're chasing a badman. There's the Indian Police forces over in the Nation, but they can't go off the land that already belongs to one of the tribes. And I told you how far it is to Fort Sill and Fort Reno."

"Well, we still have a little time to come up with some kind of plan. Maybe after I've had some sleep, I can think better."

"I hope so. And I got to do some thinking myself."

"Is there something wrong here at the C-Dot?" Jessie asked.

Dave shook his head. "No. It's Retha. On the way back here she told me she was going to marry Skip Toland. And me and Nettie are bound and determined to find a way to stop her from marrying that no-good half-breed!"

★
Chapter 11

Jessie stared at Dave with a feeling that she'd just awakened from a bad dream. She asked him, "You don't approve of Retha's choice of a husband, then?"

"Not if it's Skip Toland. He's got about the worst reputation of any man I can think of. I'll tell you something you might know already. Most bounty hunters is as bad as the scum they get paid for bringing in—or killing, which is what most of 'em had rather do, if the wanted poster says 'dead or alive.'"

"You really meant what you said to him yesterday when we ran into him up in the Quartz Mountains?"

"Doubled in spades, Jessie. Every word of it."

Nettie came in from the kitchen. Jessie said, "Dave's just told me Retha wants to marry Skip Toland, Nettie. How do you feel about it?"

"Sick to my stomach, Jessie. I can't figure out what my own little girl sees in him."

"You've talked to her, of course?" Jessie asked.

"What little I can. She ain't about to listen. I jawed at her for a long time after Dave told me last night, but she never said a word except that her mind's made up," Nettied answered.

"Would you think I was interfering if I talked to Retha?"

Jessie asked. "I'm not very much older than she is, and she might listen to me."

"I'd be obliged if you would," Nettie said. "She's in her room right now, if you're done eating." She looked at Jessie's taut face and added quickly, "And if you ain't too tired."

"I'm not that tired, Nettie. I'll rest later." Jessie got up and went to the door of Retha's bedroom. She knocked, and when Retha did not answer, she called, "It's Jessie Starbuck, Retha. May I come in for a minute?"

Retha opened the door after another wait. She looked at Jessie suspiciously and asked, "What do you want?"

"To talk with you a minute or two."

"If it's about me and Skip Toland—"

"It is," Jessie broke in. "But I'm not going to preach at you. I just want to ask you a few questions."

"Well..." Retha opened the door wider. "I guess I can stand it if you can." When Jessie entered, Retha closed the door but did not invite her to sit down. For a moment they said nothing, but measured one another with their eyes in the way women have.

Jessie's only glimpse of Retha had been an impression of dark blonde hair framing a blurred face. She had been too far away to see what was apparent now that they stood face to face. Retha was not pretty in the conventional sense. Her eyes were too small, her nose too irregular, her chin too weak, but her lips were full and pliant, her high cheekbones rosy with youth, and her skin fair and clear. Retha's figure was her best feature. Her breasts bulged full under the bodice of her dress, and her waist drew in daintily above generous hips.

Staring resentfully at Jessie, Retha put her back to the door and said, "All right. I already know what you're going to say, but talk ahead."

"What am I going to say?" Jessie asked.

"About the same thing Mama and Dave told me. I

haven't known Skip long enough to be sure about the kind of man he is, he's a no-good, he's too old for me, he's never going to be home because of the kind of work he does, he'll make me unhappy."

"You don't believe them, of course."

"They don't know Skip! I do!"

"Do you? How long have you known him, Retha?"

"Long enough. Since he did the wolfing for Dave, when we first moved to the ranch. He came back to see me a few times that Mama and Dave don't know anything about. I know him well enough to know he'll suit me fine!"

"And you don't mind that the kind of work he does makes him kill someone now and then? Or that it really will keep you apart a lot of the time?"

"Skip wouldn't kill anybody unless he had to! And Mama and Dave don't know it, but he's not going to be a bounty hunter much longer," Retha said defiantly. "He's onto something big. He'll be an important man in Greer County in a little while! The biggest man anywhere hereabouts! And he's going to be rich, too!"

"Really?" Jessie was suddenly much more interested in the girl than she had been. "How does he plan to do that?"

"He didn't tell me exactly how, and anyway, I'm not supposed to talk about it."

"Let me tell you, then. There are some very rich men from back East who are going to buy up all the land in Greer County. They'll set up their own men as range bosses and put them in as sheriff and judge and all the other county jobs, and all the men who are working for them will get rich too."

Retha's jaw dropped and she stared at Jessie with undisguised amazement. She stammered, "How—how did you know that?"

Jessie did not intend to give Retha any more details,

120

or tell her that she'd seen the cartel use the promise of power and wealth to recruit the men it needed to do its dirty work.

She shrugged and said casually, "It's an old story. Rich men are full of promises, but they don't always keep them. If I were you, I'd put off marrying Skip Toland until you see how this deal he's in works out."

Retha was silent for a few moments, staring at Jessie, then she said sullenly, "I don't care whether Skip gets to be a big man, or makes a lot of money. I love him and he loves me, and we're going to get married, no matter what anybody says!"

Jessie saw that there was no chance of changing Retha's mind at the moment. She said in a level, almost casual voice, "What you do is up to you, of course. But if I were in your place, I'd listen to what other people say, and think about it a lot before I jumped into a wedding with Toland. Now if you'll open the door, I'll leave you alone. I'm too tired to argue with you."

"Wait a minute!" Retha protested. "You've got to tell me where you found out so much!"

Jessie stared Retha down. With no sympathy in her voice, she said, "You worry about that, Retha. Now please open the door so I can go."

When Jessie rejoined Nettie and Dave, both of them looked at her expectantly. Jessie shrugged. "I don't know whether I made any impression on her. All I could do was try."

"I know you done the best you could, Jessie," Nettie said. "Retha ain't your worry, anyways. It's up to me to handle her."

Jessie told Nettie, "Give her a little time to think about what I said before you try to persuade her anymore."

"It'd help if you told us what you said," Dave suggested.

"I told her what I've found out about Skip Toland."

Dave frowned. "You didn't tell me you'd learned any more about him than what I told you, Jessie."

"No, I didn't, Dave. I held back something from you, and I'm sorry. But I had to think it through myself before telling you the rest of what I learned on Outlaw Mountain."

Quickly, because she was getting very sleepy now, Jessie sketched the details she'd omitted from her earlier account.

When she'd finished, Dave asked incredulously, "You mean Toland's the cartel's headman in Greer County?"

"I'm sure he is. He won't be for very long, of course. As soon as they've got a firm grip on things, they'll get rid of him and put someone smarter and smoother and even more Ruthless in charge here."

"What we got to do is stop 'em before they can get that firm grip, then," Dave said.

"Yes. And we don't have much time." Jessie yawned. "Time or no time, I've got to have some sleep. Maybe I can think more clearly when I've rested a little while."

Ki had no regrets about having tricked Bright Sunrise. As soon as she had left to do the chores for which she'd been hired, he began exercising his hands, flexing them and massaging them as best he could with his wrists still bound.

After experimenting for several minutes, Ki found that he could press with the fingertips of one hand on the pads of muscle at the base of the fingers of his other hand and push his wrists apart enough to get a fraction of an inch more play in the rope that lashed his wrists. With the increased mobility this gave him, the exercising went faster, but the morning was well along before his fingers regained their normal suppleness and were again under his full control.

When he had reached this point, Ki relaxed and spent

a few moments inspecting the outlaw camp minutely. He looked first for Bright Sunrise, and saw her on her knees beside the pond. She was sloshing clothes in a bucket of water, a heap of shirts and balbriggans beside her still waiting her attention. As Ki looked around the tarpaulin shelters, he saw that at several of them she had already hung wet longjohns and shirts to dry on the guyropes supporting the corner poles.

Bright Sunrise was going to be busy for some time, Ki concluded, and gave his attention to the shelter where the outlaw named Slim was sleeping. The shelter was halfway around the wall of the canyon from where Ki lay, and sixty yards of the bare rock that formed the canyon's floor lay between the two spots.

After a single quick glance, Ki discarded the idea of crossing the floor. Even if he used *ninjutsu* in moving from his present position to the sleeping man, there was always a risk that the outlaw might awaken before Ki had gotten close enough. Ki did not know how far down the access canyon the guard called Fat Joe was posted. If he was close, a shout or a shot would bring him quickly, and Ki had no illusions about the difference in range between a rifle and a *shuriken*.

Even greater was the danger that Bright Sunrise would see him, and he was not sure yet how far she could be trusted. The canyon wall would be a better approach, he decided, even though the distance he'd have to cover was twice as great.

Once he'd decided on his approach, Ki wasted no more time. He laid the thumb of his left hand across his palm and tucked it into the vee between his little finger and ring finger. Then he compressed the edge of his palm until his hand was no larger than his wrist and slid his hand out of the circle of rope that held him prisoner.

Shaking the slack loop of rope off his left hand, Ki flexed and stretched his arms until the muscles in his biceps and forearms lost their stiffness. Moving slowly to avoid attracting Bright Sunrise's attention, he turned on his side and folded his legs to bring the rope holding his ankles within reach of his fingers. A few quick tugs at the knot freed his legs.

Stretching luxuriously, Ki rippled his arm and leg muscles, tensing and relaxing them until they were no longer stiff. While he exercised, he rehearsed in his mind the plan that he was now beginning to carry out. When he decided that he was capable of making the necessary moves his plan would require, Ki stood up. He stepped back to the wall of the canyon, moving slowly, making no sudden moves that might attract Bright Sunrise's eyes.

He reached the wall and flattened himself against its rough stone surface. For a moment he stood motionless, his eyes now searching the canyon floor where it met the wall, looking for any loose stones or sudden shelving that might cause him to stumble. Satisfied that the path was clear, Ki began edging toward the shelter where the outlaw named Slim was sleeping. As he moved, he kept his eyes fixed on Bright Sunrise, who was still busy with her washing at the edge of the pond.

Ki had gotten almost halfway to the shelter where Slim was sleeping when Bright Sunrise looked up. Ki stopped quickly and met her eyes. She had her mouth open, ready to say something, when he shook his head and pointed to the shelter where Slim was sleeping. Bright Sunrise stared at him for a moment, then nodded.

Ki resumed his stealthy progress. He had almost reached the shelter when Slim sat up. Ki dropped to the ground and lay flat, hoping he'd blend with the canyon floor. Slim sat in his rumpled blankets for several moments, looking at Bright Sunrise. He stood up and, without taking his eyes off her, picked up his gunbelt and strapped it on. Then he walked over to the pond. He did not even glance at the shelter where Ki had been.

Bright Sunrise had resumed washing the shirt she'd been working on when she saw Ki. She paid no attention to Slim when he stopped beside the pond and looked down at her.

"You know, you're a right good-looking squaw," Slim said. "How about you and me having a good time while there ain't nobody else around to bother us?"

"I am working," she replied.

"You got plenty of time to finish your washing," Slim said. "And none of the others is likely to get back for a while."

"No. I have much more to do."

"Ah, come on," he urged. He fished a cartwheel out of his pocket and held it out to her. "I ain't asking you to do nothing for free. Here."

Again Bright Sunrise shook her head. She said, "I do not earn money the way you think. Please go away now, and let me do my work."

"Damned if you don't act like you're too good for me!" Slim said angrily. "Most squaws I run into's ready enough to get a good hunk of white man's meat!"

"I am not like them," Bright Sunrise said levelly, still keeping her eyes on the shirt she was washing. "I do not want you or your money. Now go away and let me work!"

"Go away, hell!" Slim snarled. "I come over and asked you didn't I? I was tryin' to be nice, even offered to pay for your time, and I don't aim to be put off! Now get up and come along with me, damn you!"

He bent and grabbed Bright Sunrise by the arm. She twisted away from him. Her movement overbalanced her and she sprawled to the ground on her back. Ki saw what the outcome must inevitably be. He rose in a crouch and began running toward the pond.

Slim leaned over and caught both of Bright Sunrise's wrists in his hands. He was just starting to pull her to her feet when one of Ki's slippers dislodged a small stone

125

that made a tiny clattering sound on the rock of the canyon floor as it skittered away. Slim started to turn his head, and Ki realized he would have to act now. He sprang, his feet leaving the ground and extending in front of him as he turned on his side in midair. Ki's heels struck Slim in the upper back, and with a loud grunt the outlaw went sprawling.

Slim was surprisingly fast, though. As Ki landed on all fours a few yards away from the hardcase, Slim was already recovering his footing and reaching for the grip of his revolver. There was no time for Ki to cover even the short distance that separated him from the outlaw, so he quickly rolled to one side, taking a *shuriken* from his vest pocket as he did so. Slim had his pistol out, and was raising its muzzle to track the lithe Oriental as Ki's hand snapped forward straight from the shoulder and released the glittering, star-shaped disc.

A smothered, gargling cry burst from the outlaw's mouth as he felt the *shuriken* bite into his flesh. He forgot the gun in his hand as blood gushed from his throat.

He stood erect for a moment, staring at Ki. Then he pitched forward on his face, the sixgun tumbling from his hand as he went down.

Bright Sunrise was still sitting on the ground when Ki got to the pond. She was looking at the dead outlaw, her features impassive, but her eyes wide with astonishment. She said, "That was not a knife you threw, Ki. If it had been a knife, he would have had time to shoot you. No knife kills so swiftly."

"It wasn't a knife, Bright Sunrise. It is a weapon of my—" Ki paused, and finished with bitterness in his voice, "a weapon from another country."

"Then in your country you must be a great warrior."

"It was my country once. It is not now."

"Ah," Bright Sunrise said. "Then are you like my

126

people? We have had our country taken from us. Are you homeless too?"

"I have a home here," Ki replied. "But this kind of talk is wasting time. We have to get away from here."

"Yes, I know this thing. Where will we go? My people are not too far from here. Would you—"

"We'll talk about that later, too," Ki broke in. "Is there another way to get out except through that long canyon?"

Bright Sunrise shook her head. "No. That's why these men use it. They are safe here as long as they guard the opening."

"I was sure that was the case. I was just hoping—" Ki stopped short. "It's all right. We'll get past the guard."

"There is only one man, Ki," she told him.

He nodded and walked to where the outlaw lay in a widening pool of blood, then bent over and wrested the *shuriken* from its lodging in the dead man's throat. He took it to the pond and washed it clean of blood, then dried it on his pants and replaced it in his pocket.

Turning to Bright Sunrise, he asked, "How long will it take you to get ready to leave?"

"I am ready now. But where will we go? To the ranch?"

"Perhaps. I'll work that out after we start. Are you sure you're ready?"

"Yes. I don't want to be here when the other men come back," she said. "They will be angry. They will know I saw this one die, and will make me tell them what happened. Then they will find you and kill you because you killed him."

"Let me worry about that."

"You speak in the way of a warrior," Bright Sunrise said. "I will gladly go with you, Ki. But do you have a horse?"

127

"No. Do you?"

"Of course. How else could I get here? It's in the corral over there, with the others."

Ki looked at the rope corral. There were four horses in it. He said, "I'll take one of theirs."

"Let us leave, then."

When he saw Bright Sunrise toss a blanket over the back of her horse and cinch it under its belly with a rope, Ki quickly decided not to waste time saddling one for himself. The thought had been growing in his mind that the day was well along, and some of the outlaws might be returning soon. Bright Sunrise was already mounted, and Ki was just readying himself to do the same, when an idea occurred to him.

"Wait," he told Bright Sunrise.

He found a lead rope hanging on a corral post and looped it around the neck of one of the remaining horses. Leading the horse and the mount he'd selected for himself, Ki went to Slim's body. Bright Sunrise followed him, a puzzled frown forming on her face. Ki lifted the corpse and tossed it across the back of the third horse. He mounted the other.

"Now we'll go," he said.

As the three horses moved slowly through the huge stone arch and entered the long canyon that cut through Outlaw Mountain, Ki told Bright Sunrise his plan.

★

Chapter 12

"Isn't Retha going to eat this evening?" Jessie asked when she came from her bedroom for supper and saw the empty chair.

"She said she wasn't hungry," Nettie replied. "But I know you must be starved, Jessie. All you had was that little pickup snack I fixed you when you got here, and you went to bed before me and Dave set down for the noon meal."

"I needed sleep more than I did food," Jessie said. She served herself with steak and potatoes from the platter Dave passed her. "Now it's the other way around. This looks good."

Dave gave Jessie a chance to get started with her meal before he asked, "Did you figure out anything about Ki, and the place where them outlaws has got him?"

"Not yet. I know that Ki won't be hurt. Skip Toland gave his gang orders not to touch Ki until he gets back from Fort Supply. And he said too, that the trip would take six days."

"That's right," Dave nodded. "Two or two and a half days going up there with an empty wagon or unloaded pack animals, four coming back with a load."

"Dave, is there any way at all we could get enough men here in six days to take that hideout?"

"I been fretting about that ever since you asked me this morning, Jessie. I just don't see no way at all."

"There must be somewhere we could go to hire some!"

"Where?" Dave asked. "There's no towns in spitting distance of here, except maybe Mobeetie, and it's a bad-man's hangout if there ever was one. Tascosa's too far, and so's that new town to the south of it they call Amarillo."

"I'd give a lot for a cannon right now!" Jessie exclaimed. "A few shots would bring down that stone arch I told you about, and it's the only opening into the hideout. If we had those outlaws bottled up, all we'd have to do is starve them out!"

"There's cannon at Fort Sill, but you know how long it'd take for the army to get 'em here. Three or four weeks, likely."

"Of course, it wouldn't have to be cannon," Jessie said thoughtfully. "Blasting powder would do as well."

"There ain't much place you'll find blasting powder around here, where there's not any mining going on. You'd have to go clear up to Colorado for that."

"Gunpowder would be just as good," Jessie went on. "It'd take a lot, of course. I remember several years ago, when the Starbuck mines up in Montana switched to blasting powder, it was because it took so much less to get the same force."

"Ten or fifteen years back, on a ranch like this I'd of had a half-dozen bags of gunpowder," Dave said. "Now-adays, it's easier to buy shells from the store."

"Dave," Jessie said suddenly, "don't I remember you saying that it's only sixty miles from here to Fort Sill?"

"If you remember me saying so, I guess I did, because that's just about how far it is."

"Until you mentioned it just then, I'd forgotten they

have artillery companies there. They'd have plenty of gunpowder."

"I guess they would, at that. But it's like pulling a horse's back teeth to get the army to let go of anything."

"I can get them to let go. I know the names to use."

"Now, Jessie, you're surely not thinking about going all the way to Fort Sill!" Nettie exclaimed. "After all you been put through!"

"What I've been through is nothing to what's going to happen to Ki unless we get him away from those outlaws before Toland gets back," Jessie told her.

"Nettie's right, though," Dave said. "Anyhow, you can't ride sixty miles there and then come back sixty miles carrying a load of gunpowder, and do it in five days."

"I don't see why not. Colonel Cody rode twice that far in half that time a few years ago," she retorted.

"That blowhard showoff!" Dave snorted. Then, his voice calmer, he added, "I know about that ride of Cody's, Jessie. He was riding between mail stations, and he changed horses five or six times. There ain't no single horse alive that can make a run like that."

"Sun can do it," Jessie said firmly. "And so can I!"

"Now, Jessie—" Nettie began.

"Don't say it, Nettie," Jessie said, a note of warning in her voice. "And don't you say anything either, Dave."

After a moment of silence, Dave said, "I guess I better not say you can't, Jessie. I've known you since you was a young'un, and I knew Alex Starbuck for a lot of years. You're his girl, all right, and when a Starbuck says they're going to do a thing, I just suspect there ain't nobody in the world can stop 'em."

"There's the curve in the canyon," Ki told Bright Sunrise. "Now, are you sure you remember what you're going to do?"

"Stop treating me like a stupid Indian, Ki. What I have to do isn't that hard to remember."

"Just act as though nothing's happened," Ki repeated. "I'll be counting from the minute you get out of sight, and when I've counted to a hundred, I'll start the horse with Slim's body on it down the canyon. When the guard sees that body, I want you as far beyond him as you can get without kicking up your horse."

"Suppose Fat Joe doesn't put his rifle down when he sees the body, the way you think he will?" she asked. "Will you be close enough?"

"I'll be as close behind that horse with the body on it as I can get without him seeing me."

"But will you be close enough?" she persisted.

"I'm sure I will be."

"I still think it would be better to shoot him. I've got Slim's rifle under my skirt. I know how to shoot it, too."

"And if there's another outlaw anywhere near, he'll hear the shot and come to find out what's happening. We can't afford to get bottled up in this canyon, Bright Sunrise."

"I understand why you're doing it this way, Ki. But I—"

"Then let's not argue about it," Ki said with finality.

Ki knew quite well the risk involved in his plan. The idea that had come to him just before he and Bright Sunrise left the hideout had seemed a good one, and workable, when he'd stopped to load the dead outlaw on the horse that he was now leading. Its flaws had occurred to him within a short time, but it remained the only scheme he could think of.

He weighed the "ifs" during the short time required for them to cover the distance to the curve that blocked the guard's sight of the stretch between it and the hideout. *If* the guard called Fat Joe was close enough beyond the curve to be in Ki's throwing range, *if* he put his rifle aside to examine the corpse, *if* he could not pick up the rifle in time to shoot before the *shuriken* reached him, *if* the star blade went true...

Ki was uncertain about only the first three. The fourth depended on his own skill. In that, he had confidence.

They reached the curve, and Ki reined in. He nodded to Bright Sunrise and gestured to indicate that she was to go ahead. She nodded and kept moving. She did not look back before she was out of sight behind the bend in the stone-walled canyon. In a few moments, Ki heard the guard's voice.

"Leavin' already, girl? Didn't take you long today."

"There was no one there to get in my way, so I finished my work early," Bright Sunrise answered.

"Well, if you got time, pull up and visit a minute. A man gets mighty lonesome, all by hisself."

"No, I have to ride on, Fat Joe. We will talk another day."

"Oh, hell, go ahead, then. The boys oughta be getting back after while, anyhow."

Ki started counting. He had in his mind a picture of Fat Joe, his back to the curve, watching the Arapaho girl's back as she rode down the long straight stretch that lay beyond the bend.

It seemed to Ki that he would never reach the end of his count. When he did, he released the lead rope from the horse bearing the corpse and gave it a kick in the hindquarters. The animal moved off, the dead man's arms swaying gently.

"What in the goddamn hell!" Ki heard Fat Joe exclaim a few seconds after the horse rounded the bend.

Ki nudged his own horse ahead and took a *shuriken* from his vest pocket. Then he was around the curve. Fat Joe was standing beside the horse, one hand on the corpse.

133

In the flash of time before he spun the *shuriken* on its deadly midair whirl, Ki saw that the outlaw had not put his rifle down, but held it in his other hand.

Fat Joe looked up and saw Ki. He brought up the gun to fire from his hip. The *shuriken* sliced into his throat a split second before the outlaw triggered the weapon. The slug missed Ki, but hit the horse. The animal reared and whinnied in a high-pitched cry of pain. Ki kicked its flanks, and the horse moved ahead, its stride broken and faltering.

Fat Joe had let his rifle drop now, and was clawing at his throat. Ki threw another *shuriken*. His target was Fat Joe's pain-contorted face, and the wicked points of the blade dug into the outlaw's cheek. Fat Joe did not fall, but let his rifle drop and brought up both hands to claw at the embedded steel stars.

Ki was only a few yards from the outlaw now. Ahead of him in the long, straight passageway he saw Bright Sunrise. She had reined in and was looking back. Ki waved to her to move on.

He came abreast of Fat Joe. The outlaw was bending double, a gabble of shrieks pouring from his throat. Ki leaned over as he passed, and brought down his arm in a *shuto* blow. The steel-hard edge of his palm struck Fat Joe's neck with the force of an ax. Lurching forward, the outlaw crumpled to the ground, his neck broken.

Ki dug his heels into the flanks of the faltering horse. It moved on, but its legs were beginning to tremble. Bright Sunrise had turned her horse and was coming back toward Ki. She had taken the rifle from beneath her full skirt and now carried it in one hand. Before she reached him, Ki's horse lunged forward and Ki leaped off only an instant before the beast collapsed, blood gushing from its mouth and nostrils.

"Get on with me," Bright Sunrise called as she pulled up her horse beside him.

Ki vaulted onto the horse's cruppers. Bright Sunrise reined the animal into a sharp turn and prodded it with her heels. It responded by breaking into a trot, but with the double load, its gait was unsteady. It weaved from one side of the widening canyon to the other as it neared the mouth, and it seemed to Ki that an hour passed before they reached the end of the confining stone passage and emerged onto the sloping flank of Outlaw Mountain.

Bright Sunrise turned to Ki and said, "We are all right now. I know the trail well from here."

"Don't take the trail!" Ki commanded. "When the outlaws come back, whether they've found Jessie or not, they'll use the trail, and we'd run into them."

Bright Sunrise said, "There are not many trails in this part of the hills, Ki. We must take one of them to get away."

"Toland took us into the mountains by another trail, close to the settlement. Do you know it?"

"Yes. But we must not go near the settlement. Toland and Perk have friends there."

"We don't have much chance to get away right now, in any case," Ki told her. "What we need is a place to hide for a while. Do you know where there's a cave, or a blind canyon?"

She pointed to the lower hills that stretched to the south. "I know canyons there. But if there are any caves, I do not know about them."

"We'll go up from here, then," Ki said decisively.

"Up? Up this mountain? But it is bare!"

"There'll be a little canyon of some kind up above," Ki told her confidently. "And if that bunch does catch Jessie, I'm going to be close by, so I can help her."

"You alone, against so many? What could you do?"

"I'll worry about that when it happens. Right now, we need a place close by where we can hide," Ki said. "Turn the horse now, Bright Sunrise. Go up the mountain. We'll have to take a chance on finding a place up above before they see us."

Bright Sunrise hesitated for only a moment. Then she tugged the reins of the tiring horse and they started up the steep slope that stretched above them.

They'd covered only a few hundred yards before it was clear to Ki that the overloaded horse could not struggle up the slope very far under its double load. He said, "Stop long enough for me to get off. I can walk as fast as the horse up this slope."

With Ki on foot, the horse made better progress. There was little vegetation. No trees grew on the mountainside, and only occasionally thin patches of low brush and groundcover sprouted from the scant layer of dry earth that spread over the mountain's stone core. Moving in zigzags that took them up the slope on a long slant, they mounted steadily until they reached a stretch of broken ground. Although Ki had never been in the Quartz Mountains before, he had seen similar terrain many times in his travels with Alex Starbuck and with Jessie.

"Pull up here," he called to Bright Sunrise. "I want to look around for a minute."

While Bright Sunrise waited, Ki began picking his way over the gully-creased slope. He'd gone only a short distance when he saw the beginning of a ledge that ran at right angles to the small crevasses that cut the mountainside from top to bottom in that area.

Ki made for the ledge. As he got closer, he saw that it was a rock shelf, and at the back of it, winds and rains and melting snow had scoured out the earth cover above the shelf to form a brow that overhung the horizontal ledge. The shelf looked solid, and was wide enough to accommodate them and the horse, with room to spare. When he stepped out to the edge and looked down, Ki could see part of the mouth of the canyon leading to the hideout, but when he moved back, the ledge hid the downslope from view.

Hurrying back to Bright Sunrise, he told her, "We'll be safe on that ledge, at least for a while. When the gang gets back from looking for Jessie, they'll start out again as soon as they find out I'm gone too. They'll head for the ranch. They won't think of looking up here."

"Of course," she nodded. "You think well, Ki. In my tribe you would be an honored fighting chief."

"We need to hide right now, not fight. Let's get the horse over to that ledge."

They'd covered only half the distance, the horse having to pick its way across the gullied ground, when a drumming of hoofbeats sounded from the trail below. With impending danger spurring them on, Ki and Bright Sunrise reached the ledge and led the horse to the back of the recess beneath the overhang. Then they lay flat on the rock shelf and looked down at the canyon mouth.

Perk was one of the riders, the outlaw named Granger the other. They rode into the canyon and disappeared. Even as far as they were from the spot where Ki's fight with Fat Joe had taken place, they could hear the loud voices of the two outlaws, but were too far away to hear what was being said. The voices died after a few minutes, and more minutes ticked off before the pair reappeared. They reined in at the canyon mouth.

"Which way you think he went, Perk?" Granger asked.

"To the C-Dot ranch, you damned fool!" Perk snapped. "Him and the Starbuck woman are both new to this country. It's the only place they know to go."

"I guess so. We sure didn't see no sign of her."

"Well, the Chinaman ain't got that much of a start. You take the trail past the settlement, Granger, I'll follow this one. Any of the boys you see, tell 'em to ride with you. The chink can't have got very far, and once he hits

137

the prairie, there ain't no place he can hide. We'll get him sure, if we hurry. Now get going!"

Stretched out on the ledge, Ki and Bright Sunrise watched the outlaws ride off. The beating of their horses' hooves died out in a few moments, and the flank of Outlaw Mountain was again a place of quiet and peace.

Nettie broke the silence that had settled over the dinner table after Jessie made clear her intention to ride to Fort Sill. She said, "Well, if you've made up your mind to do that two-day ride, Jessie, I don't guess me or Dave, either one, can stop you."

"You couldn't, Nettie. But surely you can see I've got to do it. I can't leave Ki to the mercy of those outlaws, and without that army of men Dave was saying we can't get, there isn't any other way we can beat that outlaw gang."

"I guess not," Nettie said, frowning. "But me and Dave sure will be worrying about you."

"Don't worry, please," Jessie said. "I'll make it there and back, I'm sure I will."

Dave spoke for the first time since Jessie had announced her plan. "I've had my say about it. And I won't offer to go with you, Jessie. Years tell on a man, and I got sense enough to know I just ain't up to a ride like that at my age. All I'd do is slow you up. Besides, I ain't got a horse on the place that'd be able to keep up with Sun."

"He's the best there is, Dave. He'll make the ride."

"I reckon. You don't aim to start tonight, do you?"

"No, certainly not. I'm not foolish enough to try to cross strange country in the dark. I'll leave just before daybreak. It'll be light before I've had a chance to get off the trail." She turned to Dave. "I guess there is a trail of some kind, isn't there?"

He nodded. "Such as it is. The army engineers done

some grading in the high spots during the War, when they was hauling cannons all over everyplace."

"Will I hit any rough country?"

"It ain't too bad. There's some little hills and humps, but it's mostly plain old flat prairie."

"Are there any landmarks to look for?"

"None to speak of. The country won't give you no trouble, Jessie. Just ride back to the Sweetwater Fork, the way you come in. It's low at this time of year. Bear a little south after you cross, and you'll pick up the trail."

Nettie, practical in the way of women at such times, said, "You'll need to eat good and keep up your strength. I'll fry up some steak, and I've got plenty of fresh bread from the baking I did the day before you got here. There's a spare canteen around someplace. I'll brew a batch of good strong tea and fill it up."

"Even if I don't like your idea, Jessie, I'll do what I can to help," Dave offered. "What'll you need besides food?"

"Oats for Sun," Jessie said promptly. "I'll go out and look at his hooves and make sure they're in good shape. It was an easy ride here from the railroad, though, and I'm sure he's all right. I've got horse liniment in my saddlebags, just in case."

"You stay in here and rest up," Dave said. "There's plenty of oats in the shed, and I'll give Sun a good rubdown, see he's in good shape and all."

"I appreciate it, Dave. And what you're doing too, Nettie. I—well, I just don't have the words to tell you."

"Not that you need none." Dave stood up. "You go get your rest, Jessie. You'll need it, and starting fresh will help. Let Nettie and me do whatever's needed to get things fixed up."

Jessie went back to her room and stretched out on the bed. The weariness she'd brought back from Outlaw Mountain had already been banished by her earlier rest.

She lay quietly, thinking of Ki in the hands of Toland's gang, putting aside any thoughts of the grueling ride that lay ahead. When worry over tomorrow began nagging at her, she closed her mind to it and soon went to sleep.

★

Chapter 13

After the two outlaws had left, the echoes of their horses' hoofbeats fading as they took their separate trails, Ki told Bright Sunrise, "It looks as if we'll be safe until it's dark enough for us to leave."

"Yes. And since no one will see us here, we can enjoy the time we have." Bright Sunrise got up and went to her horse, took off its saddle blanket, and spread it on the ledge below the overhang. "This will be better than lying on the rock. Come and share it with me."

Ki went and lay down beside her. For several minutes they lay side by side in silence, then she asked, "Didn't you understand my invitation, Ki?"

"I'm here with you, Bright Sunrise. What other invitation was there?"

"Among my people, a woman as well as a man can invite someone to share a bed. Don't I please you, Ki?"

"Of course you do."

"Then take my invitation."

Kit turned to face Bright Sunrise. She was looking at him with a mixture of anticipation and anxiety. He said, "You really mean it, don't you?"

"Since I felt the medicine of your strength and gentleness the night you found me watching the big horse, I

141

have waited to invite you. If I hadn't meant it, would I have asked?"

"No, of course not." Ki ran his fingertips down her cheek and took her chin in his palm. "I'm not used to your customs, and your invitation was a surprise."

"Is it a good surprise, Ki?"

"Very good."

Ki leaned forward, and Bright Sunrise moved to meet him. Their lips touched, a bit hesitantly at first, then Bright Sunrise darted her tongue out, Ki opened his lips and met her tongue with his, and their halfhearted touching became an embrace.

Bright Sunrise was less uncertain than Ki. While their kiss was still gaining intensity, her hand slid down his chest, her fingers opening and closing on the taut muscles they encountered. She slid her palm along Ki's taut stomach and let it come to rest on the bulge at the front of his denims.

Ki's hands were busy too. He released Bright Sunrise's chin, stroked her strong, sturdy neck, and passed his palm down her smooth shoulder. She turned her body slightly to let his fingers slip under the low, loose neck of her blouse. She was wearing nothing under the blouse, and he found the nipples of her firm, upstanding breasts. She began to shiver as Ki's steely fingers rubbed her rosettes, and he felt their tips spring to life.

Under his jeans, Ki's erection was just beginning to grow. Bright Sunrise rubbed her hand along it, squeezing gently now and then on the swelling flesh. Soon it was not enough for her to feel him only through the layer of cloth that separated skin from skin. She released him long enough to find the buttons of his trousers and open them, allowing him to spring erect without the hindrance of the cloth.

They ended their kiss at last, both short of breath.

Bright Sunrise sat up, leaned over Ki, and looked at him with shining eyes. "You are hard now everywhere I feel you, Ki. And big, as a man with such powerful medicine should be."

Ki did not answer. He had slipped her blouse down to bare her breasts, and was caressing them, rolling her nipples between his steely fingers. Her body grew taut as he continued his caresses, and her quickening breath turned into a chorus of soft, humming sighs, and her hand closed tighter on his erection.

Bright Sunrise whispered, "Now I invite you again, Ki. But hurry, do not make me wait any longer."

She pushed the waist of her full skirt down past the swell of her hips and kicked the skirt aside. Throwing a leg across Ki's hips, she twisted below him as he turned to her and leaned above her. She still held his rigid shaft tightly in her hand, and now guided it between her spread thighs.

Ki entered her with slow deliberation, enjoying the rising tide of her slick, warm flesh on his shaft. Bright Sunrise arched her back and squirmed as he went deeper, lapsing into her native tongue, uttering words he did not understand as she lifted her hips to meet his almost leisurely penetration.

"What are you telling me, Bright Sunrise?" Ki whispered.

"To hurry, hurry, hurry! And how big you are, how fine and hard, and how much I like feeling you in me."

To please her, Ki drove in forcefully, full length, with a single powerful lunge. She gasped, a smothered half-scream. Ki could not tell whether it was a cry of pleasure or pain, but he pressed firmly against her, his hips spreading her thighs apart, while Bright Sunrise clasped her arms around his neck and found his lips and thrust her tongue between them.

Ki lifted his hips and drove again, and then again, and she broke their kiss, her head rolling and tossing on the rough blanket. She was laughing and moaning at the same time, and as Ki changed the tempo of his moves and began stroking in a steady rhythm of long, deliberate thrusts, her cries grew louder and burst from her throat each time their bodies met.

As Bright Sunrise's moans became gasps and her hips began to grind against his, Ki realized that she was near a climax. He did not ease up to delay it. He lengthened his strokes and lunged even harder while her gasping changed to high, shrill screams and her body trembled. At last she shrilled a final cry of ecstasy and tossed in a wild, climactic spasm. Her passion subsided slowly, the twitching of her muscles ended, and she lay quietly, inert, her body now a warm pillow for Ki's muscular frame.

Ki did not move, but lay still himself, buried deeply in her.

"You fill me as fully as you did at first," Bright Sunrise said after a few more minutes passed. She slid her hand between their bodies and Ki felt her finger pressing on his shaft. "You are still hard!" she exclaimed.

"Does that disappoint you?"

"No." Her denial was hesitant, almost a question. Then she went on, "Did I not please you, or do the men of your race feel nothing when they are in a woman?"

"You pleased me a great deal, Bright Sunrise. And I don't know about all men of my race, but I enjoy pleasing a woman more than once."

"You feel as ready as you were before!"

"I am. Are you?"

"Yes, oh, yes! Start now, and don't stop until you have had your pleasure too!"

Ki began thrusting again. This time he did not move with slow deliberation, but pounded with quick, trip-hammer lunges that brought Bright Sunrise to a climax within moments.

When her gasps and groans diminished to a soft, breathy sighing, he slowed the speed and vigor of his strokes. He let himself build when she began to respond once more, and this time he did not hold back. As Bright Sunrise thrashed and quivered beneath him, Ki reached his own peak. To the accompaniment of her waning moans, he throbbed again and again, and when Bright Sunrise went limp and lay with closed eyes, he lowered himself on her soft, receptive body and let himself relax also.

After a long soft silence, Bright Sunrise whispered, "Now I know I have pleased you." She stirred, and Ki moved to leave her, but she clasped him tightly and went on, "No. I like you this way too. Stay with me. Sleep, if you want to."

"We can't afford to sleep," Ki told her. "Have you forgotten the outlaws?"

"For a while I did," she answered, smiling.

"So did I." Ki smiled too, for a moment. Then his face grew serious and he said, "Maybe we'd better separate, Bright Sunrise. They won't be looking for you. The only two who knew you were at their hideout are both dead."

"No, Ki. I stay with you."

Her tone left no doubt in Ki's mind that Bright Sunrise was serious, but he still resolved that he'd try to persuade her. He kissed her softly and raised himself. Bright Sunrise sighed as Ki stood up, then accepted their separation and stood up herself. Ki walked to the edge of the shelf and looked along the trail that led from the hideout.

"By now, Perk and his men must be on their way back," he said. "When they didn't see me crossing the prairie, they must have figured out I'm around here somewhere, and this time they'll do a better job of searching. I don't like to think of what they'll do to you if they find us together."

"They wouldn't think of looking for us if we went east."

"Is there a trail to the east? If there is—"

"There is an old trail that the Kiowas and Comanches once used," Bright Sunrise said thoughtfully. "I have never been over it, but I have heard of it."

"Do you think we can find it?"

"We can try. But it will take us a long time to go around the mountains, with only one horse."

Ki looked up at the conical peak of Outlaw Mountain rising above their heads. He said thoughtfully, "Maybe it would be easier if we just circled around the mountain."

"But there's not any trail!"

"We don't need a trail. The ground's fairly smooth. All we need to do is stay above the hideout until we pass it, then begin to go downhill a little at a time. When we get to the other side, we'll be right on the prairie."

"Do you really think that will fool them?" Bright Sunrise asked, frowning.

"I think it's our best chance," Ki replied. "When the gang comes back, they'll scatter again to search around here, and that will give us time to get to the C-Dot."

Bright Sunrise looked up and studied the peak again. Trying to hide the doubt in her voice, she said, "If you think it is best to climb Outlaw Mountain, Ki, I will go with you."

Jessie set out from the C-Dot when the first faint line of false dawn showed along the rim of the eastern horizon. She raised her hand in a goodbye salute to Dave and Nettie, who stood silhouetted against the yellow lamplight streaming from the open door of the ranch house, and then she turned Sun to the east.

Rested and well fed, the big palomino was frisky, as good horses are in the early morning. He wanted to gallop across the dew-wet grass, but Jessie held him back with a firm hand, saving his strength for the time when it would be needed more. Sun took the gentle reining-in a bit reluctantly, tossing his head each time she twitched the reins to restrain him.

In addition to Jessie's slim young body, the palomino was carrying a light load, not enough weight to strain a horse of such size and breeding. Jessie had emptied her saddlebags and put aside everything that would add even an ounce of weight, then packed them with the essentials for her trip. As she'd remarked to Dave, her chief concern was the trip back, when the gunpowder would be added to Sun's burden.

Now, tucked in among the bags of oats that Dave had filled the night before, carefully distributed so the weight on each side would be equal, the saddlebags held only a folded nosebag, the food Nettie had prepared, a bottle of horse liniment, two bandannas, the small deerskin pouch containing the gold coins she carried as a reserve fund, and ten spare rounds for her special Colt .38/.44, which rode in its holster on Jessie's hip.

Still, the saddlebags had seemed very heavy when she'd thrown them over Sun's rump behind the saddle. After a great deal of thought, she'd decided not to take her rifle, and had even left behind the derringer she'd learned to depend on as a backup weapon.

Daylight arrived with startling speed. The false dawn's glow persisted only briefly; within a few moments the true dawn pushed it aside, and soft morning gray filled the sky for a short while. The gray increased swiftly in brightness, then it was suddenly dyed the lustrous orange that heralded sunrise and persisted until the sun rose and flooded the prairie with its harsh brilliance.

For the next two hours, Jessie rode with the sun in

her eyes. No matter how low she pulled the wide brim of her Stetson, no matter how far down she bent her head, the sun was there, sending the promise of a bright warm day. After a while, Jessie gave up the uneven fight to shield her face, and rode with slitted eyelids, closed so far over her smarting, watering eyes that she could see the high, waving prairie grass in front of Sun's head only as a blur of tan.

By noon, Sun's friskiness had worn off. He was still fresh, but now his long strides were measured and businesslike as he kept to the mile-eating gait Jessie set. They had crossed the shallow Salt Fork of the Red River in midmorning, and Jessie had made her first stop there to drink a few swallows of the tea from her canteen. She'd let Sun drink as sparingly as she did; there were other streams ahead, where the water was better.

After the Salt Fork crossing, Jessie set the palomino on a slant to the south, to miss the north bend made by the horseshoe curve of the Red's Sweetwater Fork. "You been over that part of the ride before," Dave had reminded her when they were talking about her route at the lamplit breakfast table. "You go south a bit, and miss that west bend of the horseshoe. That saves you crossing twice, and you'll pick up the first stretch of what's left of the old army road just on the east side of the river."

Jessie was no stranger to uninhabited land. The Circle Star was located in one of the least-settled areas to be found, but as she rode she was struck by the differences between the land surrounding the Starbuck ranch and that which she now saw.

In Southwest Texas, the land was arid and vegetation sparse. Here the grass grew lush and tall, belly-high to Sun as his sturdy legs covered mile after mile. It was rich country she was crossing now, country that would support three or four times the number of steers per acre that the Circle Star was capable of grazing. Seeing it in all its endless unsettled expanse, she did not wonder that Greer County was coveted by both Texas and the Indian tribes, as well as by the old Starbuck foe, the cartel. It was a rich prize, promising wealth to whoever finally got it.

In the early afternoon, Jessie reined Sun to a halt on the bank of the Sweetwater Fork. She swung off his back, her legs stiff after almost ten hours in the saddle. The palomino did not seem tired, and she let him drink his fill. Then she dug bread and meat out of the saddlebag and ate while she strolled around to work the stiffness out of her legs.

A scant quarter-hour of rest was all that she allowed herself. In the saddle again, she let Sun pick his way across the river. A hundred yards from the bank, a stretch of low-growing grass marked the beginning of the abandoned military road. Jessie pulled the palomino onto the strip, but after a mile, when Sun had stumbled and broken stride several times when he stepped into one of the deep ruts hidden by the creeping grass, she went back to the prairie.

There were no landmarks in sight when darkness came, and the featureless terrain offered no suggestion of shelter. Jessie had been riding all afternoon with only her lengthening shadow on the grass in front of her. The shadow served as a compass, and kept her moving in the right direction.

In the last gray shadow of dusk, Jessie pulled up. She tethered Sun and let him cool off while she unsaddled him and ate quickly. Then, before spreading her blanket, she filled the nosebag with oats and let the palomino eat. She knew that during the night he would graze lightly, so she did not refill the bag.

While the horse ate, Jessie unrolled her blanket and

found a spot free of humps and bumps to spread it out. She went back to Sun and took off the nosebag, poured into it enough water to satisfy his thirst, and when he'd snuffled up the last of the liquid, she turned the bag over to drain and dry. With her boots tucked under her saddle and the saddle itself for a pillow, she stretched out on her blanket and quickly went to sleep.

Jessie did not wake until the rising sun struck her face. She opened her eyes and blinked at the bright light, realizing with a sudden surge of anger that she'd over-slept. She was about to spring to her feet when she felt a strange pressure against her thigh. Lifting her head a bit, she peered down her body. A rattlesnake was cuddled close to her, its string of rattles at her waist, its body stretching beside her to its triangular head at her feet.

Jessie froze. She was snake-wise, for rattlers were common around the Circle Star. She realized that the rattler had sought warmth during the cool night, and had slithered beside her so quietly that its movement had not awakened her. She knew, too, that in spite of the legend, a rattlesnake could and would strike without coiling, and that she was safe only as long as it did not feel her moving.

Her Colt, still holstered, was lying on the blanket near the snake's tail. Moving with infinite care, Jessie stretched her left hand out and picked up the revolver. She did not try to take it from its holster with her left hand, but transferred it to her right hand and worked it from the holster. With the same care, Jessie extended her left hand again until it almost touched the snake's rattle-tipped tail.

Taking a deep breath, Jessie acted in one quick flash of motion. She closed her hand on the tail and in the same instant jumped to her feet, swinging the rattler in a circle above her head. Three swings gave her enough momentum to toss the snake a dozen feet away, and as

150

it landed on the tall grass, a quick shot from her Colt blew off the rattler's head. Only then did Jessie release the breath she'd been holding since she reached for the snake.

By now the sun had cleared the horizon and was beginning its climb up the sky. Jessie fed Sun and let the horse drink while she made her own breakfast of steak and bread, with cold tea from the canteen. She saddled the palomino, rolled her blanket and tied it on with the saddle strings, replaced the saddlebags, and was on her way again.

This morning she let Sun gallop a bit to make up the time she'd lost by sleeping late. For about ten minutes of each of her first three hours on the trail, she gave the big horse his head and reveled with him at the rush of wind against her face as his mighty strides cut down the distance at a quick rate.

Noon was near when they reached the rough country that stretched to the Wichita Mountains. She saw from a distance that these were prairie mountains. In a land where flatness is the rule, almost any hill comes to be called a mountain.

While the Wichitas, like the Quartzes, had no imposing peaks, the land for a score of miles around them was rough and broken, studded with outcroppings of red sandstone. Here the army road beside which Jessie rode swung to the south. Looking at the road and at the chopped-up terrain ahead, Jessie made a quick decision. She kept Sun moving on a straight line and rode into the rough terrain that lay ahead.

Nearing the end of the broken country, with the prairie visible ahead, Jessie regretted her decision bitterly. The great palomino had been forced to move more slowly when they entered the uneven terrain, and Jessie had let the horse set its own pace. The golden horse had responded by keeping to a fast walk, though the ground rose and fell, and high sandstone ledges forced him to detour around them.

He was skirting such a detour, crossing a low, flat sandstone ledge that lay almost flush with the surface of the soil, when his hoof came down on a thin section of the porous, fragile rock. The rock cracked and broke under the impact of his iron-shod hoof, and the hoof plunged through. Sun staggered and tried to regain his balance, but his hooves slipped on the unyielding surface. Jessie felt him going down, kicked her feet out of the stirrups, and jumped. Sun fell heavily, and lay still.

★

Chapter 14

Jessie landed on her feet on the sandstone and skidded for a moment, her arms flailing. She kept her balance, and ran to Sun. The palomino's head was twisted cruelly, and for a moment Jessie was seized by a feeling close to panic at the thought that the great horse she loved so well was dead. Then Sun moved and whinnied unhappily, and straightened out his neck. He did not try to get to his feet, and Jessie's heart sank again.

"Quiet, Sun," she commanded. The horse answered her with a whinnying snort and let his head down on the ground.

Jessie went around the fallen animal and felt the foreleg that had gotten trapped. Her fingers told her nothing. She dropped to one knee, lifted the injured leg gently, and rested the hoof on her knee. Interlacing her fingers, she encircled the pastern and ran her hands slowly up the fetlock and over the joint to the cannon.

As her hands moved up Sun's leg, she pressed hard with her thumbs, and felt better when she'd reached the knee without feeling the sharp, ragged, telltale edge of a broken bone. Still, she was not satisfied. She shifted her position and supported the leg with the horse's knee on hers. Filled with the dread of what she might hear, she grasped the pastern and twisted Sun's leg. The palomino whinnied when he felt Jessie's hands on him, and she thought she heard pain in the sound. She twisted harder, working her hands in opposite directions, and still there was no play, no looseness, no grating of bone on bone.

Sighing with relief, Jessie laid the leg down and stood up. She went to Sun's head and knelt to press her cheek against the golden hair of his nose and rubbed the velvet of his muzzle.

"You'll be all right, Sun," she said. "It's not broken, but I'm sure it's pretty badly sprained. Come on, get on your feet and let me see what I can do."

Gathering the reins, Jessie tugged them gently upward. "Up, Sun," she said. The palomino did not respond at first, and Jessie repeated her order. "Up, now. Good horse, Sun. Get up, boy. Up! Stand, Sun!"

Sun rolled to get his feet under him, and heaved himself up. He stood on three legs, the knee of the injured foreleg bent, his hoof dangling. Jessie could see that the leg was beginning to swell just above the fetlock joint. She let the reins drop and went to Sun's forequarters and pushed the leg down until the hoof touched the ground. He leaned a bit to take his weight off the hoof, but left it on the ground.

Sun was not the first horse Jessie had treated. Digging into her saddlebags, she found the bottle of liniment and the stout bandage she'd had the foresight to bring. Pouring liniment on the injured leg, she rubbed it in well, then poured more on and rubbed again. Sun still kept his weight off the leg. Jessie bandaged it from knee to pastern joint, pulling the heavy cloth taut but not tight.

Tying the bandage off, she picked up the reins. Under ordinary circumstances, on home pasture, she would have let a horse with a sprain stand until it moved of its own volition. Telling herself these were not ordinary circumstances, Jessie set her jaw and tugged the reins gently.

For a moment Sun refused to move, but Jessie praised him and encouraged him by keeping a light but steady pressure on the reins. Gingerly, Sun tried a forward step. He tried to walk on three legs, and almost went down again, but regained his footing after giving Jessie a few anxious seconds. Then, in response to her continued urging, he stepped cautiously ahead.

Jessie led him around for a moment or two, then started ahead. Sun followed, limping. She walked him for an hour, stopping occasionally to let him rest his leg. When he was walking without hesitation, but still limping, she halted long enough to saturate the bandage with more liniment, then swung into the saddle. Sun flinched, but did not whinny. Jessie touched his flank with her booted toe. Limping badly, Sun moved slowly off.

As the long afternoon wore along, Jessie alternated riding for a few minutes and walking, leading Sun. Lacking the flow of fresh air created by riding, Jessie sweated. Big drops ran from her forehead into her eyes and down her cheeks, and dripped off her chin. For a while she mopped her face with the bandanna she carried, but it soon grew soggy and unpleasant. She used her sleeve instead, but when it became too wet to be effective, she stopped wiping and let the perspiration drip.

Sun moved more and more slowly as the day faded, until by sunset Jessie no longer tried to ride. She stopped from time to time to let the big palomino rest and to rest herself. She gave him water at one of the stops, and twice poured fresh liniment over the bandage. Her own feet were throbbing and had swelled uncomfortably inside her boots, but she was afraid that if she took them off it would be impossible to get them on again. The prospect of being totally immobilized was worse than the pain. She trudged on, Sun following.

Darkness was near when she reached a little stream,

and Jessie's spirits soared. In the western part of the Indian Nation, rivers and creeks were so rare that she knew she must have gotten to Cache Creek. She stopped, not sure whether Fort Sill was upstream or down from where she stood. A short distance downstream, there was a rise in the bank where the creek had cut through one of the last low foothills of the Wichitas.

Picking up Sun's reins, moving more slowly than ever because the palomino was now limping worse than at any time since his fall, she headed for the rise. From the top she saw buildings, and men in gray field uniforms walking between them. The distance was little more than a mile. Wearily she led Sun along the bank of the creek toward Fort Sill.

Ki and Bright Sunrise were making slow but steady progress along their chosen escape route around the flank of Outlaw Mountain. They'd gotten off the ledge without much difficulty. Backtracking for a few yards past the beginning of the ledge, they reached a spot where the way was clear for them to climb straight up the steep mountainside until they were well above the overhang. Bright Sunrise's pony had not liked the climb, but with Ki hauling on the lead rope, they'd reached the point where it seemed safe enough to start moving horizontally on a slow downward course.

Ki had in mind a clear picture of what their route should be, a spiral around the mountainside that would allow them to descend gradually as they circled, until, on the flank opposite the hideout, they would arrive at the foot of Outlaw Mountain where it joined the prairie. The only trouble with his plan was that the mountain refused to cooperate.

Thus far, Ki had only been on the southern side of the mountain, and he'd judged the entire formation by what he'd seen. Shortly after he and Bright Sunrise started their gradual descent, they reached the northern flank.

Though the winters in Greer County were almost as dry as the summers, the summer rains were seldom accompanied by high winds. This was not true of the winter storms. They often brought gale-force winds, which had driven the rain and sleet against the unprotected slope.

Cascading down the steep flank over countless years, the rushing water had gouged great gullies in the soft soil. It had left huge piles of loose gravel on the upslope side of any boulder or hump of stone or other obstruction. At places the roiling water had stripped away the soil in great patches, leaving bare the quartz-studded granite core of the mountains.

Alone, Ki and the Arapaho girl could have managed to make their way around the northern flank. Leading a half-broken Indian pony, whose weight started fresh slides in the loose dirt and whose hooves slipped on the exposed granite, the job was more difficult than Ki had thought it would be.

"I guess my idea wasn't a very good one," he confessed as they stopped to rest after crossing an especially difficult spot. "At the rate we're going, it'll take us two days to get around."

"Shall we turn back, then?" she asked. "Maybe at night we can go to the trail without Perk and the others hearing us."

Ki looked at the sky and shook his head. "We can't. Before we got there, it would be dark. The gang would be in the hideout by then, and you know how sound travels at night."

"It's the horse that slows us down," Bright Sunrise said. "By ourselves, we'd have no trouble."

"We need the horse to get across the prairie. They may have left some of the gang to watch the trail. With

157

the horse, we've got a chance to get away from them on level ground. We couldn't do it on foot."

"What will we do, then, Ki?"

"About the only thing we can do," he said, managing a smile in spite of his frustration. "We'll go ahead."

Jessie thought she'd never reach the fort. Sun was hobbling with increasing difficulty, stopping each time he lifted his hoof to let the injured leg rest, and whinnying with pain when he placed the hoof on the ground. The bandage on the leg was bulging, and the flesh above it swelled. One painful step at a time, Jessie and the big horse moved along the creekbank. The sun had set and the windows of the buildings were aglow when one of the soldiers saw Jessie and came up to her.

"Looks to me like you need some help, miss," he said. "Can I give you a hand?"

"My horse is in worse shape than I am," Jessie replied. "If you'll show me the shortest way to the stables, there must be someone there who can take care of him."

"Sure. We got a real good horse doctor here. And the way you're limping along, I guess you could use some doctoring too. Now let me take them reins, and you lean on me. The stables is just a little ways off."

Ten minutes after Jessie reached the stables, a veterinarian was examining Sun's leg. He stood up after feeling and prodding the swollen fetlock joint with his fingers and manipulating the hoof, and came to where Jessie stood watching.

"Your horse will be just fine in three or four days, ma'am," he told Jessie. "He's just got a sprain. All he needs is to stand a few days and let his leg rest. And I'm sure you could use some rest, too. In four or five days, a week at most—"

"I don't have four or five days," Jessie interrupted. "I'm going to start back tomorrow."

"Not on that palomino, ma'am, unless you want to cripple him for life, maybe have to shoot him."

"I'd better talk to your commanding officer, then. Where can I find him at this time of day?"

"Colonel Cordell? Is he a friend of yours?"

"No. But that's not important."

"Well, the colonel's gone to his quarters by now, ma'am. He doesn't take kindly to being disturbed after retreat. But in the morning—"

"Now!" Jessie said imperiously. "Will you show me the way, or shall I ask someone else?"

For a moment the veterinary officer hesitated. Like most army veterans, though, he'd learned to recognize authority when he encountered it. He said, "Well now, if you put it that way, ma'am, I'll be glad to escort you."

Colonel Cordell was a short man, small in stature. As she looked down at his suntanned face, adorned with the official Burnside beard of the mounted services, Jessie was sure that on a horse he'd be much more impressive. Summoned from his supper over the objections of his orderly, he stood with a napkin in his hand, glaring at her and the veterinary officer.

"You're in violation of standing post orders, Lieutenant!" he snapped at the veterinary officer, then turned to Jessie and said, "Miss . . . Starbuck, you said? Miss Starbuck, it's our duty to help you civilians, of course, but since what you call an emergency doesn't involve an attack by hostiles, it can wait until morning. I'll see you in my office tomorrow and listen to your story."

"Colonel Cordell," Jessie said in a voice that had the hardness of chilled steel, "if you expect to retain your command of this post, within the next ten minutes you will send a message on the army telegraph to Secretary Ramsey in Washington, telling him that Jessica Starbuck has requested your assistance, and ask him for instructions. If you don't send that message, I'll wire him myself and tell him you refused to help me when I asked you to."

Colonel Cardell's eyes widened. He looked at Jessie again, examining her grimy face, dirt-streaked, sweat-stained blouse, and equally stained jeans.

"Are you telling me that you're acquainted with the Secretary of War, Miss Starbuck?" he asked.

"I'm sure you know that Secretary Ramsey's home is in Minnesota," Jessie said quietly. "I have some business interests there, mining, lumber, railroads. I also have some friends in Washington who advised President Hayes to offer Alexander Ramsey his appointment as secretary."

Cordell's eyes slitted, and Jessie knew that he was debating whether or not she was bluffing, trying to decide whether to call her bluff. She decided to push a little harder.

"I know it's late, Colonel," she went on. "Mr. Ramsey won't be in his office, but there are messengers on duty twenty-four hours a day at the War Department. They'll know that Secretary Ramsey's home address is 801 K Street. That's ten minutes from the department's offices. It will take you two hours or so to get an answer to your wire, and I'm prepared to wait that long."

Unofficially and quietly, Cordell surrendered. "I don't think it will be necessary for me to send a telegram, Miss Starbuck," he said, forcing a semblance of interested cordiality into his voice. "I'm sure you wouldn't ask for our help unless you had a real need for it. I'll be glad to do whatever I can."

"Thank you, Colonel," Jessie smiled. "Now, what I need—"

"Just a minute, Miss Starbuck," Cordell broke in. "From your appearance, what you need most right now is some rest and a good meal. Mrs. Cordell and I are just sitting down to dinner. If you'd care to be our guest, we can talk about your problems while we eat."

"That's very kind of you, Colonel." Jessie could afford to relax now, and her smile was not forced, but genuine. "I'd be delighted."

Ki and Bright Sunrise huddled closer together and tried to pull the horse blanket tighter around them to shut out the thin night wind that was blowing up the side of Outlaw Mountain. Their progress up hill had been slower than they'd thought it would be, and darkness had caught them before they'd reached the end of the eroded area that had defied their efforts to cross it.

"I'm sorry I got you into this, Bright Sunrise," Ki said. "You could be warm and comfortable at the C-Dot right now."

"I'd rather be here with you, Ki."

"We may be here longer than we'd planned. Unless we move faster than we've been able to today, we'll still be trying to get down to the prairie this time tomorrow."

"No. Your medicine has been powerful enough to help us escape from Perk's gang and get us this far. It will carry us the rest of the way."

"I know we'll get on around the mountain," Ki said. "What I'm thinking of is the time it's taking. Jessie and I need time to plan a way to handle Toland and Perk and their crew."

"You haven't told me about Jessie, Ki. Are you with her all the time?"

Ki caught the hint of jealousy in her voice. He said, "Your tribe is the Arapaho, Bright Sunrise. Jessie is my tribe."

"And that is all?"

"That's all." Ki took Bright Sunrise in his arms. "And we are here together. If it's not too cold—"

Bright Sunrise cuddled closer to Ki, and her hands

161

began to explore his body. "Even if it was colder than this, it would not matter. Make me warm, Ki!"

"You're sure that this will be better than gunpowder?" Jessie asked the ordnance sergeant. She picked up one of the slim cylinders and examined it more closely, rubbing her hand along its slick wrapping of thick red paper. "It's not much bigger than a candle, Sergeant. How can it be as powerful as you say it is?"

"Take my word for it, Miss Starbuck," the sergeant replied. "That Swede who figured this new dynamite out sure knowed what he was about. We been trying it out some this past month, seeing it's so new and all. I tell you, when it goes off, whatever's close to it is going to get busted up."

"And you're sure it will break up a thick slab of solid stone?"

"We ain't tried it on anything yet that it wouldn't bust. We set off just one stick of it in an old cannon that's stood up to double charges of gunpowder, and it busted that barrel into a thousand pieces."

"And it won't go off in my saddlebag?"

"It's safe as houses," the sergeant assured her. "You can throw it or hammer on it, but the onliest way you can set it off is the way I showed you, with a cap and fuse."

"And this fuse will burn a foot a minute?"

"Give or take a few seconds. Just make sure you allow time to get enough space between you and whatever you're blasting."

Jessie was already packing the dynamite and fuse into her saddlebag. The day was just beginning, but after a full night's sleep in a comfortable bed in Colonel Cordell's own quarters, she felt refreshed and ready to start back. Picking up her saddlebags, she walked across the ordnance shop to where Cordell stood waiting.

"I'm ready to leave, Colonel," she said. "And I thank you very much for being so helpful."

As they went out the door, Cordell said, "My pleasure, Miss Starbuck. I wish I could provide an escort, but our orders are very strict. Unless there's Indian trouble, not a single man wearing the U.S. uniform is to set foot in Greer County."

"I certainly wouldn't ask you to disobey orders," Jessie said dryly as they stopped beside the cavalry horse that Cordell was lending her from the fort's remount station. "And I wouldn't think of asking Secretary Ramsey to make an exception in my case. I'm sure he'll understand that when he reads my telegram." She threw the saddlebags over the animal's cruppers and began tying them with the saddle strings.

"Don't worry about your horse," Cordell told her. "I'll see that he gets the very best care."

"I'm sure you will." Jessie patted the neck of the chestnut that Cordell had lent her. "This is a nice animal, but I know I'll miss Sun."

"Can't say I blame you. He's a magnificent animal."

Just as Jessie swung into the saddle, an orderly came up and handed a folded telegraph flimsy to the colonel. He unfolded the flimsy and scanned the message, then looked up at Jessie.

"One more thing, Miss Starbuck," he said. Jessie raised her eyebrows questioningly. Cordell went on, "Secretary Ramsey asks me to give you his very best wishes, and he wants you to be sure to visit him and tell him the outcome of your problems in Greer County the next time you're in Washington."

"I'll do that, Colonel," Jessie nodded. "And I'll see you again within a very short time, I hope."

As Jessie wheeled the chestnut gelding, Cordell saluted. She waved goodbye, dug her heels into the gelding's flanks, and started on the long ride back to the Quartzes. A smile crept over her face as she looked back and saw Cordell still watching her. In spite of herself, Jessie was beginning to like the crusty little martinet.

★

Chapter 15

Jessie felt a surge of relief when the roofs of the C-Dot's main house and its outbuildings broke the monotonous line of the horizon. They were still far from her, at least another hour of hard riding, but the end of her long trip was now in sight.

She'd been afraid, almost from the minute she rode out of Fort Sill, that the cavalry chestnut was no match for Sun in speed and stamina, and her fears had proved justified. The animal was not as large as Sun, and consequently had smaller muscles, which reduced both its power and endurance. Sun could keep going hour after hour without getting tired, but the remount horse was used to frequent rest stops.

In addition, the chestnut had been squadron-trained, and horses undergoing this training were used to galloping all-out for only the distance of a battle charge, usually less than a mile. Squadron training also conditioned an animal to move at a speed set by the slowest horse in a unit. As a result, those capable of greater-than-usual speed over long distances were not accustomed to using their full potential on a long, single-horse, cross-country ride.

Slowed by the chestnut's bad habits, Jessie's return trip took three days instead of the two she'd spent on the way from the ranch to Fort Sill. She welcomed the sight of the C-Dot's buildings, and urged the chestnut to pick up speed, for the animal had been slowing perceptibly as the afternoon wore away. The buildings gained height and bulk as she drew closer, but when she was still four or five miles from them, she began frowning.

Her frown was caused by much more than the blinding rays of the setting sun that now shone full on her face. A pair of packmules, led by a man on a dappled horse, were approaching the C-Dot. At that distance, with the sun behind him and in her eyes, Jessie could not make out any details of the rider's appearance.

At her first glimpse of him, she'd jumped to the conclusion that the horseman was Skip Toland, since he'd been leading two mules when he left the hideout, heading for Fort Supply. At that point a nagging worry had begun growing in her mind, but she brushed it aside, reminding herself that Toland was not due back for still another day.

Jessie kept watching the rider as their courses brought them closer together, positive that whoever he was, he was not Toland. She was close enough now for some details of his appearance to be visible in outline, but while his face was still a vague blur, there was a nagging familiarity about him that bothered her. The man had on a dome-crowned derby with a narrow brim, a city-dweller's hat. He also wore a dark suit.

Now, as the distances diminished, Jessie divided her attention between the strange horseman and the ranch house. The stranger was much nearer to the C-Dot than Jessie was; he would reach the house within a matter of five or ten minutes. Jessie could not hope to cover the remaining distance in much less than a half hour.

As the C-Dot's main house grew larger, Jessie saw something else that gave her an unpleasant shock, and reinforced the foreboding that had been nagging at her since she'd first sighted the mysterious stranger. Reason joined instinct now to convince her that there was something very wrong at the C-Dot.

Two horses stood at the hitch rail in front of the house. One was piebald gray, and Jessie knew it was not one of Dave's horses, nor was it one she'd seen elsewhere since reaching Greer County. She had seen the other horse before, and at very close range. It was the showy paint pony that Toland had been riding on the day he took her and Ki through the Quartz Mountains.

Counting in her mind the days since Toland had left, Jessie assured herself she must be mistaking Toland's horse for another that looked like it. The bounty hunter had been very specific when she'd overheard him telling Perk and the outlaws that he would be gone six days, and on her own trip to Fort Supply, she'd just learned how difficult it was to cut time off a long ride.

Seeing the animals was more than enough to urge Jessie to hurry. She compressed her lips and kicked the chestnut harder than she had before. The horse responded with a burst of speed, and when it reached the point where its training had conditioned it to slow down, she kicked it again. The chestnut hesitated, then picked up its pace until it was running at an all-out gallop once more.

Before Jessie had covered half the distance to the C-Dot, the stranger had reached the ranch house and dismounted. He went inside, and in a moment Dave Clemson emerged from the front door, the stranger following him. Dave untied the lead rope from the city-garbed man's horse and waited until the stranger had mounted it. Then, with the unknown man trailing him closely, Dave led the mules around the house and toward the corral.

Jessie could not tell from their actions whether Dave or the other man had seen her, but she took no chances.

She was getting close enough to be recognized at a glance, so with a gentle tug of the reins, she turned the chestnut until she was riding at an angle to the C-Dot, giving anyone who'd been watching her the impression that she was heading away from the ranch instead of going toward it. The maneuver would cost her a little time, but it would give her an opportunity to try to figure out exactly what was happening.

Jessie was sure her ruse would be successful. For the first time she was glad she was not riding Sun, for the palomino would have been a dead giveaway. When she'd first recognized Dave, she'd still been so far from the C-Dot that recognition had been possible only by the manner in which he moved. It wasn't likely that any stranger glancing at her would think she was more than a passing rider. She suddenly realized that while she'd been absorbed in watching the ranch house, the chestnut had slowed down. She dug her heels in the animal's flanks, and it reluctantly picked up speed again.

During the time she'd been chafing at her helplessness, Jessie had closed half the distance to the C-Dot. Though she could no longer see the front of the house, the hitch rail was separated from the veranda far enough still to be visible, and she had no doubt now that the paint pony was Toland's. She took her eyes from the horse when the stranger in the city clothing reappeared between the house and the barn.

Jessie dropped from the chestnut quickly and stood behind it, peering over the horse's back to watch the man. For an instant she got a glimpse of his face in profile; he had a nose that curved into a hook, like a hawk's bill, and he wore a black beard. It was a face she'd seen before, a brief glimpse in the open doorway of the house where she and Greg Hendricks had been held captive in San Antonio.

Jessie wondered what had happened to Dave while

the stranger reined in at the corner of the veranda and raised his voice, calling to someone inside. When he called, he turned his head away from Jessie, and all she could hear was a jumble of garbled sound.

A moment later, a second strange man came into sight, walking from the house to the hitch rail. Unlike the first unknown, he wore rancher's garb. He went to the hitch rail and untied the piebald, mounted it, and turned the horse away from the house. The man who had been leading the packmules rode up to join him, and the two started across the prairie in the direction of the Quartz Mountains. Now, Toland's paint pony stood alone.

As soon as the two men had their backs to her, Jessie remounted and started again. She rode parallel to the house until she was hidden by the barn. As soon as there was no longer any danger that she might be spotted by anyone in the main room who happened to glance out a window, she reined the chestnut around, kicked it to get a final burst of speed, and headed straight for the barn.

Pulling up at the back of the barn, Jessie dismounted. She drew her Colt and began walking quietly toward the kitchen door.

There was no veranda at the back of the house, just a low stoop. As Jessie tiptoed across the boards, she heard the sound of voices from the house, but could not understand what was being said. She reached the door and began turning the knob a fraction of an inch at a time. The door was not locked. She eased it open slowly and carefully. It was Toland's voice she'd heard as she crossed the stoop, and now she could hear him clearly.

"...a damned good thing I was cagy enough not to tell anybody where I was really headed," the bounty hunter was boasting. "If I hadn't gone to Mobeetie instead of Fort Supply, I wouldn't have got back here till tomorrow. I'd of been too late to get ahold of the Jap and the redskin girl, or the Starbuck woman either, and

169

I guess amongst the bunch of you, you'd of had a right hot reception all ready for me, wouldn't you?"

There was silence while Toland waited for an answer, but neither Ki nor Dave replied. Jessie could almost see Ki's impassive face, staring through the half-breed renegade as though he did not exist.

Toland realized after a moment that he would get no response from his captives. He raised his voice and called, "Retha! Hurry up! I wanta be away from here in time to get to the Quartzes before it's full dark!"

"I'm just about ready."

Retha's voice was muffled a bit by distance. Jessie decided the girl must be in her bedroom. She pulled the kitchen door open a bit farther, to create a crack wide enough to let her peek inside. Through the open archway that separated the kitchen from the main room of the ranch house, she saw four chairs in a line near the dining table. In them sat Ki, Bright Sunrise, Dave Clemson, and Nettie. Both Ki and the Arapaho girl were tied up.

All that Jessie could see of Skip Toland was his right hand, in which he held a revolver. Toland's face and body were out of her sight behind the edge of the arched passageway.

Jessie studied Ki's bonds. Several strands of rope were looped around his chest and arms and around the back of the straight chair. His slippered feet were held fast by loops around his ankles. A glint of light on the table at Ki's side caught Jessie's eye; they were Ki's *shuriken*.

Looking again at Dave, Jessie saw that he did not have on a gunbelt; she glanced at the rack inside the front door and saw the gunbelt hanging there, Dave's S&W in its holster. His rifle was on the pegs above the rack.

Retha came in from the wing where her bedroom was located. She was carrying a lady's carpetbag. She said, "I'm all ready, Skip. We can start now."

"Retha!" Nettie protested. "You're not going off with this man after what he's done to us, are you?"

"You hush, Nettie!" Toland snapped. When Nettie subsided, he said to Retha, "We ain't leaving yet. I told you I was going to stay here till that Starbuck dame gets back."

"Then why were you telling me to hurry?" she asked.

"Because I need you to help me. Put that satchel down and go out in the barn and get me some rope."

"What are you going to do?" Retha asked, her voice fearful. "You're not going to tie Mama up, are you, Skip? You told me you wasn't going to—"

"Never mind what I told you! Scat after that rope, now! From what you said, that Starbuck woman's way late getting back here, and I want these three tied up good and tight before she shows up."

"Now, Skip, you promised me you wasn't going to hurt Mama!" Retha protested. "You're not going to—"

"Shut your mouth and do what I tell you to!" Toland's voice was harsh.

Retha put her carpetbag on the floor and started toward the kitchen door. Jessie did not stop to close the door, but ran as fast as she could to get to the barn before the girl came out. She'd barely reached its open doors and ducked inside before she heard Retha's footsteps on the wooden stoop. She holstered her Colt and stood waiting in the gloomy interior.

Retha came into the barn. She was blinking, peering into its dark interior, when Jessie stepped behind her and seized Retha's wrist and twisted her arm up into the small of her back. At the same time she clamped the palm of her free hand over Retha's mouth.

"Now keep still and listen to me!" Jessie hissed, her mouth close to Retha's ear. "If you don't know what Toland's got in mind for your mother and the others in there, you're a bigger fool than I think you are! Can't you see he's got to kill them?"

Retha twisted her head around, trying to look into Jessie's eyes. She tried to shake her head, but Jessie was holding her mouth and chin too tightly. A garbled rattle of sound came from Retha's throat, but when she realized that as long as Jessie held her, she could say or do nothing, she stopped trying to talk. She did manage to shake her head a fraction of an inch in reply to Jessie's question.

"Are you trying to tell me you won't yell and bring Toland out here?" Jessie asked.

This time Retha tried to move her head to nod. Jessie took a chance and removed her hand from the girl's mouth.

Retha gasped for breath, then said, "Skip swore he wasn't going to hurt Mama, Jessie. I told him I wouldn't have nothing more to do with him if he did."

"Toland's a killer and a liar, Retha," Jessie said coldly. "You know he's already murdered two men. Do you think he's just going to kill Ki and me, and leave the rest of you alive to testify against him in court when he's caught?"

Retha said stubbornly, "He promised me—"

"Toland would promise anything to get his way, Retha. What makes you think his word's any good?"

"Skip loves me! He wouldn't do anything that'd hurt me!"

Jessie swung the girl around so that they stood face to face, and released her wrist. "All right. Go ahead, if you think Toland cares all that much about you."

"What—what do you mean?" Retha stammered. She started to say something, stopped, and then repeated, "Skip loves me!"

"If you're so sure of that, if you trust him all that

much, then take him the rope he sent you after and let him tie up your mother and the others," Jessie suggested.

Retha's jaw dropped and she stared at Jessie. "You— you don't mean that I—"

"I mean that you can do what you want to," Jessie said. "I won't lie to you, Retha. I intend to stop Toland, if I can."

"But if you're going to—" Retha began.

Impatient with the girl's slow-working mind, Jessie broke in and said, "Listen to me closely, Retha. If you take that rope into the house, I'll be right behind you with this in my hand." She drew her Colt. "But remember, you'll be in front of me. If Toland wants to kill me—which you know he does—he'll have to shoot you first. Now do you feel like betting your life against mine that he won't kill you to get at me?"

Retha's eyes bulged, their whites clearly outlined in the dusk of the barn's interior. She stared at Jessie without speaking while she tired to find an answer. As Jessie had hoped when she spelled out what was likely to happen, Retha was beginning to understand the real character of her lover.

Finally, Retha managed to say, "The way you put it, Jessie, I ain't real sure now what Skip'd be likely to do."

"I've given you a choice," Jessie told her impassively. "If you value your mother's life, or your own, you'd better make up your mind. Toland's been waiting a long time for you to bring him the rope he sent you to get."

As though Jessie's words were his cue, Toland's voice came from the house in a shouted command. "Retha! Get in here with that rope! Hurry up, dammit!"

"Well, Retha?" Jessie asked.

Her voice still showing her reluctance, Retha said, "I guess I don't want to take a chance, Jessie. What do you want me to do?"

While Retha had been reaching her decision, Jessie had been planning ahead. She said crisply, "Take Toland the rope."

"But I thought—"

Not unkindly, Jessie said, "Don't think about what I'm going to tell you to do, Retha. Just do it."

Meekly, Retha nodded. "All right. Just tell me what."

"Take the rope in," Jessie said, speaking slowly. "He'll tell you to tie up Dave and your mother and the Indian girl."

"How do you know he will?" Retha asked, a worried frown creasing her forehead.

"Because I've known men like him before." Jessie's patience was wearing thin. Her voice sharp, she repeated, "Take the rope to Toland. He'll tell you to tie the others up. When he does, throw the rope to him."

Retha had learned her lesson. She nodded, then asked, "And what should I do then?"

"Fall down on the floor. If you're in his way, Toland might hit you when he starts shooting."

"You're sure—" Retha began.

Jessie interrupted quickly, "I'm sure he'll *try* to shoot, at least. There's a coil of rope hanging on that peg by the door. Take it in to Toland."

Retha obeyed. She lifted the heavy coil off the peg and started for the house. Jessie waited only a moment before following her. She was only a step behind Retha when the girl went into the kitchen. As soon as Jessie was inside she dropped flat on the floor and began crawling toward the arch leading to the main room. Retha was a step or two ahead of her.

"Well, it took you long enough!" Toland growled when Retha went into the main room. Jessie was in the arched opening by then. The bounty hunter went on, "Loosen up that coil and tie up Dave. Then tie the Indian

174

girl. Then I'll—" His words broke off in an inarticulate grunt as the heavy coil of rope hit him in the chest.

Jessie was on her feet by then. Toland saw her, but Retha had forgotten to fall down. She stood between Jessie and the bounty hunter. Toland pushed Retha aside. The few seconds he needed to get her out of his way and the heavy rope that had hit him delayed his movements. As Retha moved, Toland swiveled his gun hand, trying to bring the weapon around to fire at Jessie.

Jessie shot first. Her slug caught Toland in the chest and the bounty hunter staggered back a step. He had his weapon trained on her by then. Jessie had known from the first that she could not escape being a target. She dropped back to the floor, firing again as she went down.

Toland's gun hand was sagging by the time his finger closed on the trigger. The heavy slug from his .44 scattered splinters from the planks as it ripped into the floor a few inches from Ki's slippered feet. Then Toland's hand opened and the pistol slipped from his nerveless fingers and dropped, his body covering the gun as he crumpled to the floor.

After the gunfire, the silence in the room was overwhelming. Retha broke it with her sobs as she dropped to her knees beside the dead bounty hunter. Nettie came out of her shock when she heard Retha crying, and went to her side. Dave stared sadly at the two women.

Ki was the first to speak. "For a while, I didn't think you were going to get here in time, Jessie."

"Maybe it's just as well that I didn't get here any sooner," Jessie replied. "How did Toland manage to take charge here, Ki? And, come to think of it, how did you get here? You were tied up on Outlaw Mountain when I left."

"Bright Sunrise helped me get away," Ki explained. "Toland was waiting when we got back from the hideout.

It's my fault that he captured me. I was careless. I didn't expect him back from his trip so soon."

Ki did not explain in detail how he'd managed to escape from Perk and his men, and Jessie did not ask why he and Bright Sunrise had come back together from the Quartzes.

Dave said, "Toland come to the ranch to get Retha, Jessie."

Retha looked up when she heard her name mentioned. "Yes, and if you and Mama hadn't talked so much against him, we'd have been gone before that woman got here and killed him!" She stared at Jessie and went on, "Damn you, Jessie Starbuck! I wish I hadn't listened to you out in the barn! It's your fault—"

"Hush, Retha!" Nettie commanded sharply. "If anybody's to blame, it's me for raising you up to be such a fool!"

"You hated Skip, too!" Retha sobbed. "You and him"—she pointed to Dave—"you and him are the fools! Skip was going to be the biggest man in Greer County, not just a little old—"

Nettie slapped Retha across the mouth. "You shut up! Come on, I'll get you out of here before you make more of a fool of yourself!"

Grabbing Retha roughly by the arm, Nettie dragged her out of the main room and into one of the bedrooms, slamming the door behind them.

"Do you want to go help Nettie, Dave?" Jessie asked.

Dave shook his head. "Me being there would just make Retha worse. You seen how little use she's got for me."

"I'm sorry," Jessie said. "If there's—"

Dave broke in, "You know you can't help, Jessie. And all I can do is wait and see how things turn out." He took a deep breath and went on, "Now, I was about to tell you. When Toland come here, he had them two other men along, fellows I never seen before, and one of 'em come in with him. I tried to keep Retha from leaving, but Toland drawed on me. He had his gun in his hand when Ki and Bright Sunrise got here, so they just walked into it. He made me tie Ki up, and—"

"What about the other man with Toland, Dave?" Jessie asked. "Did he ever come in the house?"

Dave shook his head. "He stayed outside. Just before you showed up, he come to the door and said they better get a move on before it got too dark. He acted like he was Toland's boss or something. That's when Toland told the other fellow to take him and start out, said he'd bring the stuff out with him and Retha. I was worried about Nettie so bad that I guess I didn't pay as much mind to watching as I ought to've done."

Ki said, "Neither of those men was with Perk's gang the other day, Jessie. The only clue I got was when Toland called the man who was in here by name. He called him Willets."

Jessie thought for a moment and shook her head. "It doesn't mean anything to me right now, Ki. I saw both men when I was riding up, but they didn't appear to notice me. I did get a good look at one, though."

"Maybe they didn't get a good look at you, Jessie," Ki said thoughtfully. "Or maybe you were too far away for them to recognize you. I know one thing. The man who stayed outside most of the time wasn't from around here. He wore city clothes."

Jessie nodded. "That's the one I got a good look at, Ki. He's the man you tried to catch in San Antonio."

"Are you sure?" Ki asked. "Because if it's the same man, that means he's been trailing us for days."

"Yes. And I'm sure he's the one Toland called 'the boss.'"

Dave broke in to say, "I got a hunch you're right, Jessie. Before Ki and Bright Sunrise got here—"

Jessie looked at the Arapaho girl. "You're Bright Sunrise, I suppose?"

"Yes. I work for Mrs. Clemson. And I know you are Jessie."

"Bright Sunrise has been a lot of help to me," Ki said quickly. "I'll tell you about it later. Let Dave finish now."

"I ain't got much more to say, Ki," Dave said. "Toland told Retha he had some important business going on and he wanted her to come along, because he might not be getting back to the ranch for a spell."

"It all comes together, doesn't it?" Jessie asked Ki. "You know how the cartel operates. They wouldn't trust a man like Skip Toland with anything important, they'd want their own men to be in charge. After Toland did the rough work, this man with the one they call 'the boss' would step into Toland's shoes, and be their front, and the boss would work through him."

Ki nodded. "Yes. We've both seen the pattern, Jessie."

"And this time we've got a chance to get our hands on one of the cartel's chiefs," she said. "I'm sure he's come here to check up on what Toland's done. That means he's probably on his way to the hideout right now. Ki, we've got to capture that place before he has a chance to get away!"

"Bright Sunrise and I got out of the hideout," Ki said quietly. He didn't mention that he'd had to kill two of the outlaws to do so. "It should be easier to get in than out."

Jessie shook her head. "We'd be fools to go in looking for a gunfight, Ki. The odds against us are too high. What we'll have to do is to seal the canyon they use going in and out. They'll give up after they get hungry enough."

"You make it sound awfully simple," Ki said with a

wry grin. "But I suppose you've got it all figured out."

"I have. It won't exactly be easy, but we can do it."

"Go ahead," Ki invited. "Satisfy my curiosity."

"Didn't Dave tell you why I went to Fort Sill?"

"No. In fact, I didn't know you had."

"We didn't have no time to visit when you and Bright Sunrise got here, Ki," Dave said. "Toland seemed to know you was gone, though. I guess we all know who told him."

Jessie nodded and then said quickly. "That's not important now. Ki, I went to Fort Sill to get some gunpowder. I had the idea that we can pick a time when all the outlaws are in the hideout and blow up that arch at the mouth of the box canyon. There's enough stone in it to seal the opening, and from what I saw of it the other day, there's no place on those walls where they can climb out."

"I can guarantee there's not," Ki assured her. "I studied every inch of the canyon sides, looking for a place to climb them. You're right, Jessie. We should be able to seal it by blowing up that arch."

"If we can do it while the cartel's man is in there, and trap him with the others—" she began.

"We might find out some things we've wanted to know for a long time," Ki finished for her. "But that's a very big piece of solid rock, Jessie. It's not going to be an easy job."

"I brought back what we need to do it," Jessie said.

"Gunpowder?"

"No. A new explosive. It's called dynamite."

"I've heard of it." Ki frowned. "It's made of nitroglycerin and clay. It's supposed to be twenty times as powerful as blasting powder. That's what you brought back from Fort Sill?"

"Yes. The army's testing it there, and the commander

179

let me have some. The man who's doing the testing said it's more than enough to blow up the arch."

"Then let's go blow it up," Ki said calmly.

Jessie and Ki set out across the dark prairie, riding side by side. Jessie had refused Dave Clemson's offer to go with them, in spite of his urging. Ahead, visible only as irregular black silhouettes against the starlit sky, rose the low peaks of the Quartzes, dominated on the north by the much higher rise of Outlaw Mountain.

When they'd gotten a mile or more from the ranch, Jessie said, "We don't know how long it's going to take us to handle the job we're getting into, Ki. Let's gallop while we're still on this flat prairie."

"I've never known you to do something unless you had a good reason, Jessie. You set the pace, I'll keep up."

They galloped until they reached the barren area where the prairie gave way to the first rise of the foothills. Jessie slowed their pace then, and asked, "Do you remember the way, in case I get turned around?"

"You won't, but I do," Ki said. "I suppose you've been thinking about what's ahead, as I have?"

"Yes. It's not going to be the pleasantest job we've had to do, Ki. But you agree it has to be done, don't you?"

"Of course. And I think this is the only way to handle it."

Both Jessie and Ki recognized the point where they'd left the trail to scout the rim of the canyon leading to the hideout. They reined in the horses and turned them up the slope, walking the animals now, until Jessie halted.

"This is far enough. We'll have to leave the horses here. I don't imagine Perk's changed the position of the lookout post, and they're too noisy to take any closer."

They took the dynamite, fuse, and box of caps from

Jessie's saddlebag and started along the rim of the access canyon. Moving silently through the darkness, they reached the point where the canyon began its curve into the hideout. They stopped to listen, and after a few tense moments they heard the scrape of boots on the stone floor as the lookout changed positions.

Ki uncoiled the *surushin* that he wore around his waist and handed it to Jessie. She lowered one end over the canyon rim, the iron ball at one end pulling the strong, thin rope straight, the ball at the opposite end providing her with a grip-stop.

Jessie braced her feet. As silently as a ghost, Ki lowered himself over the wall until he could drop to the canyon floor. His rope-soled slippers made no sound as he started toward the lookout.

Jessie heard the outlaw on guard give only a small, smothered grunt when Ki attacked. Another few moments passed and then Ki was back, groping for the end of the *surushin*. Jessie felt him grasp it, and she held tight while he used the rope to help him mount the sheer rock wall.

"He won't give an alarm," Ki said quietly.

They moved on along the rim until they saw the glow of the outlaws' fire on the box canyon's floor. In that country, where wood was scarce, the fire was so small that from where they stood on the rim, they could not distinguish the faces of the men gathered around the little blaze.

"You'd better go take a look while I cut the fuses and put them in the dynamite," Jessie told Ki. "Let's make sure we've got the men we want in our trap before we spring it. But don't forget to look back this way now and then."

"I won't forget. I'll be watching you, Jessie," Ki said.

Bending low, Ki started around the box canyon's rim. Jessie took her penknife from the pocket of her jeans and began cutting the coil of stiff fuse cord into equal lengths. She handled the padded box containing the caps gingerly as she placed it on the ground and opened it.

Kneeling, she carefully fixed a cap to one end of each length of fuse. She had begun cutting slits in the sticks of dynamite, in which to insert the capped ends of the fuse, when the hard muzzle of a pistol jabbed into her back.

"Don't move," the man holding the gun grated. "I'd as soon not have to pull the trigger on you, but I will if I have to."

"You won't have to shoot me, Dave," Jessie said quietly. "Ki and I have been expecting you."

Dave Clemson whirled a second too late. Ki's muscular arm had already started encircling his throat, cutting off any shout that Dave might try to utter. At the same instant, Ki clamped the steel-hard palm of his other hand over Dave's gun hand, immobilizing the hammer of the revolver that Dave had been pressing into Jessie's back.

Ki maintained the cruel pressure on Dave's throat until the onetime foreman of the Circle Star sagged into limp unconsciousness. He lowered Dave to the ground, bound him with the *surushin,* and gagged him with a bandanna from his pocket.

"You were right, of course," he told Jessie. "But it was hard for me to really believe we were right about him until I saw him sneaking up on you a minute ago."

"I had a hard time convincing myself," Jessie said. Her voice was sad. "I didn't realize how hard it must have been for Dave, all the years when he watched Dad becoming more and more successful, then, after Dad was murdered, having to take orders from me. I'm sure Dave still thought of me as just a little girl, and felt I hadn't earned the right to take over."

"He had me fooled until today, when Toland didn't

tie him and Nettie up after he'd surprised Bright Sunrise and me at the ranch. When did you start suspecting him?"

"Not until I was riding to Fort Sill," Jessie replied. "I had a lot of time to think while Sun was covering all those miles, Ki. Suddenly I realized that from the day Toland held us at gunpoint, there'd been a false note in the way he and Dave treated each other. I thought some more, and saw that the cartel wouldn't put a crude man like Toland into any important position. Dave was another matter. He'd had all those years working with Dad and me. He'd be very valuable to them."

"Yes. I can see that. Do you think he's done us much harm already, passing on information?"

Jessie shook her head. "He hasn't had time, I'm sure. But we'll find out more about that later. What did you see down in the hideout?"

"They're all there. Perk, the outlaws, and the two we're most interested in, Willets and the one who's bossing things, they're both down there."

"Then let's get these sticks of dynamite in place and seal the hideout," Jessie said crisply.

Ki bundled the dynamite into his arms and began inching his way across the top of the arch to the opposite side of the canyon. Jessie paid out the coils of fuse as he moved, twisting the stiff, unruly cord to keep it straight.

She glanced over her shoulder at Dave from time to time. Soon after she and Ki began setting the dynamite, his eyes opened and he began struggling to free himself. Jessie kept watching, and when Dave looked up and saw her, he dropped his head and refused to meet her eyes. After a while he gave up his useless efforts to break free, and lay quiet.

Across the arch, Ki searched the stone with his fingers to find splits and fissures in its surface, and carefully placed the sticks of dynamite in them. He set three sticks at the point where the arch ended, two more in its center, and three at the end where Jessie stood. Ki finished his job quickly and came back to Jessie.

Jessie took a small bundle of matches from her blouse pocket and handed several of them to Ki. Kneeling where Jessie had laid the ends of the fuses, they touched matches to the cords. The fuses shot streams of sparks as they caught, and Jessie jumped up.

"We'll have to get Dave away too," she said. "You grab one arm, I'll take the other."

With Dave between them, unsure of his balance with his arms bound, they ran up the side of Outlaw Mountain, away from the canyon rim. They were fifty yards upslope when Dave stumbled and fell. As they helped him to his feet, he twisted away from their hands and began running down the mountainside. Ki started after him. Jessie grabbed his shirt and pulled him back.

"No, Ki!" she cried. "The dynamite will explode in the next few seconds! We'll go after him later!"

They watched Dave stumbling down the mountainside, saw him lose his footing and fall to the ground. He rolled toward the edge of the canyon and reached it just as the fuses burned down to the dynamite.

With a staccato series of ear-splitting blasts, the dynamite exploded. Flashes of red flame darted up from the canyon rim. They saw Dave's body, a black shape against the white-hot blast, tumbling down into the mass of stone when the arch collapsed into a heap of massive blocks.

Jessie and Ki were blinded by the flashes. Instinctively they closed their eyes. They heard the grinding of the great chunks of granite falling to seal the box canyon, a soft sound compared to the blast that had preceded it.

Shouts were coming from the outlaws in the hideout. Jessie and Ki opened their eyes, and their night vision slowly returned. They looked at the jumbled, massive stone blocks that now sealed the box canyon, but there was no sign of Dave.

"He's dead, of course," Ki said soberly. "Maybe it's for the best."

"Yes," Jessie agreed. "We've still got the two cartel men in the hideout. They can tell us more than Dave could have."

They walked to the edge of the box canyon. Two of the outlaws were throwing more wood on the fire. It blazed up brightly, and Jessie saw the cartel's man, a stranger in city clothes among the group that milled around the fire.

Jessie shouted, "You men listen to me! Don't try to fight us! You're trapped in there and you know it!"

A few of the outlaws drew pistols, but let them sag when the cartel man drew their attention by running for his horse. He leaped on its back and started at a gallop toward the sealed opening. The horse balked when it reached the piled heap of stone blocks. For a moment the man from the cartel stared up at Jessie. She saw his face clearly for the second time, the sharp hawk nose and black beard clear in the firelight.

Taking a derringer from his pocket, he put the muzzle to his head and pulled the trigger. His body slumped and slid slowly from the horse's back.

Not only Jessie and Ki, but the outlaws in the hideout fell into a stunned silence that was broken almost immediately by the drum of hoofbeats coming around the slope of Outlaw Mountain. They came to a halt, and a handful of men rushed up to the rim, where Jessie and Ki stood silhouetted by the firelight. They were dressed as roughly as the outlaws, their clothing dusty and travel-stained. Jessie stepped forward to greet a short, small-boned man who emerged from the nondescript group.

"I'm sorry we couldn't wait for you, Colonel Cordell," she said as he saluted her. "I wasn't sure when you'd get here, and we had to move fast."

"We got a late start. I had to make out furlough papers for all these volunteers, as the Secretary instructed. Then we rode in forced marches," Cordell said. "And we've been floundering around in the dark for the past half hour, in spite of your excellent map. If it hadn't been for the blast, we'd still be looking for this place."

Jessie looked at the men who'd just arrived, and smiled. "No uniforms, I see."

"Of course not." A frosty grin split the colonel's face. "We'll put our uniforms on when we get back, before we take our prisoners to jail."

"Ki and I will leave them for your men to handle, then," Jessie said. "And we'll visit with you overnight when we come to get Sun on the way home."

"He'll be ready, Miss Starbuck," Cordell said. "And it'll be a pleasure having you as my guest again."

As Jessie and Ki rode around the slope of Outlaw Mountain to the trail that led to the prairie, Ki said, "You always manage to have a surprise for me, don't you, Jessie?"

"You surprise me as often as I do you, Ki. We'll get caught up on what happened to both of us after we finish our unhappy job at the C-Dot, while we're riding home. And I'll be very glad to be back at the Circle Star. We can relax there for a while, because I have a feeling that after this, the cartel won't be ready to make a move for quite a while."

In companionable silence broken only by the clumping of their horses' hooves, Jessie and Ki rode down the slope to the prairie, away from Outlaw Mountain.

Watch for

LONE STAR AND THE GOLD RAIDERS

twelfth in the hot new
LONE STAR series from Jove

coming in June!